PRAISE FOR RUBEM FONSECA

"Fonseca's work confirms, in the final analysis, that as a writer he has gone where none have dared in Brazilian literature."

—*World Literature Today*

"Fonseca's narratives take advantage of, and reinvent, existing popular literary forms, such as the crime novel, but also the political, social, existential, and erotic novel."

—2003 Juan Rulfo Prize Jury

"Fonseca's books (*High Art*, etc.) are like the movies of Spain's Pedro Almodóvar: they take an infectious, comic delight in the solemnity of popular fiction (whether thriller or melodrama, on page or on screen) without exhibiting solemnity themselves."

—*Publishers Weekly*

THE TAKER

and Other Stories

RUBEM FONSECA

*Translated from the Portuguese
by Clifford E. Landers*

OPEN LETTER

LITERARY TRANSLATIONS FROM THE UNIVERSITY OF ROCHESTER

First hardback edition, 2008
First paperback edition, 2022
All rights reserved

"Angels of the Marquees" originally appeared in *Ellery Queen's Mystery Magazine*; "The Book of Panegyrics" originally appeared in *The Literary Review*; "The Other" originally appeared in *Review*; "Night Drive" originally appeared in *Ellery Queen's Prime Crimes 5*; "Trials of a Young Writer" originally appeared in *Two Lines*; "The Flesh and the Bones" originally appeared in *Words Without Borders*.

Translation of these stories was made possible by a 2004 grant from the National Endowment for the Arts.

Library of Congress Catalog-in-Publication Data: Available.
isbn-13: 978-1-948830-70-6 / isbn-10: 948830-70-x

Printed on acid-free paper in the United States of America.

Text set in Bodoni, a serif typeface first designed by Giambattista Bodoni (1740–1813) in 1798.

Design by N. J. Furl

Open Letter is the University of Rochester's nonprofit, literary translation press:
Dewey Hall 1-219, Box 278968, Rochester, NY 14627

www.openletterbooks.org

CONTENTS

NIGHT DRIVE

I ARRIVED HOME with my briefcase bulging with papers, reports, studies, research, proposals, contracts. My wife, who was playing solitaire in bed, a glass of whiskey on the nightstand, said, without glancing up from the cards, "You look tired." The usual house sounds: my daughter in her room practicing voice modulation, quadraphonic music from my son's room. "Why don't you put down that suitcase?" my wife asked. "Take off those clothes, have a nice glass of whiskey. You've got to learn to relax."

I went to the library, the place in the house where I enjoy being by myself, and, as usual, did nothing. I opened the research volume on the desk but didn't see the letters and numbers. I was merely waiting. "You never stop working. I'll bet your partners don't work half as hard and they earn the same." My wife came into the room, a glass in her hand. "Can I tell her to serve dinner?"

The maid served the meal French style. My children had grown up; my wife and I were fat. "It's that wine you like," she said, clicking her tongue with pleasure. My son asked for money during the coffee course; my daughter asked for money during the liqueur. My wife didn't ask for anything—we have a joint checking account.

"Shall we go for a drive?" I asked her. I knew she wouldn't go—it was time for her soap opera.

"I don't see what you get out of going for a drive every night, but the car cost a fortune, it has to be used. I'm just less and less attracted to material things," she replied.

The children's cars were blocking the garage door. I moved both cars and parked them in the street, moved my car from the garage and parked it in the street, put the other two cars back in the garage, and closed the door. All this maneuvering left me slightly irritated, but when I saw my car's broad bumpers, their special chrome-plated double reinforcement, I felt my heart race with euphoria. I turned the key in the ignition. It was a powerful motor that generated its strength silently beneath its aerodynamic hood. As always, I left without knowing where I would go. It had to be a deserted street, in this city with more people than flies. Not the Avenida Brasil—too busy. I came to a poorly lighted street, heavy with dark trees, the perfect spot. A man or a woman? It made little difference, really, but no one with the right characteristics appeared. I began to get tense. It always happened that way, and I even liked it—the sense of relief was greater. Then I saw the woman. It could be her, even though women were less exciting because they were easier. She was walking quickly, carrying a package wrapped in cheap paper—something from a bakery or the market. She was wearing a skirt and blouse.

There were trees every twenty yards along the sidewalk, an interesting problem that demanded a great deal of expertise. I turned off the headlights and accelerated. She only realized I was going for her when she heard the sound of the tires hitting the curb. I caught her above the knees, right in the middle of her legs, a bit more toward the left leg—a perfect hit. I heard the impact break the large bones, veered rapidly to the left, shot narrowly past one of the trees, and, tires squealing, skidded back onto the asphalt. The car would go from zero to sixty in less than seven seconds. I could see that the woman's broken body had come to rest, covered with blood, on top of the low wall in front of a house.

Back in the garage, I took a good look at the car. I ran my hand lightly over the unmarked fender and bumper with pride.

Few people in the world could match my skill driving such a car.

The family was watching television. "Do you feel better after your spin?" my wife asked, lying on the sofa, staring fixedly at the TV screen.

"I'm going to bed," I answered, "good night everybody. Tomorrow's going to be a rough day at the office."

THE TAKER

On the door there was a large set of dentures with Dr. Carvalho, Dentist, underneath. In the waiting room was a plaque: *Wait for the dentist, he is with a patient.* I waited for half an hour, my tooth aching. The door opened, and a woman came out. She was with a large guy, maybe forty years old, in a white jacket.

I went into his office, sat down in the chair. The dentist put a paper napkin around my neck. I opened my mouth and said my back tooth was hurting a lot. He looked at it with a little mirror and asked how I had allowed my teeth to get into that condition.

What a laugh. These guys are funny.

"I'm going to have to pull it," he said. "You've already lost a few teeth and if you don't undergo treatment fast you're going to lose all the others, including these here," and he gave a strident tap on my front teeth.

Anesthetic injected into the gum. He showed me the tooth at the tip of his forceps. "The root is rotten, see?" he said, indifferently. "That'll be four hundred."

What a laugh. "I don't have it, man," I said.

"You don't have what?"

"I don't have the four hundred." I started for the door.

He blocked the door with his body. "You'd better pay," he said. He was a large man, and he had large hands and strong wrists from pulling teeth out of so many fucked-over *fodidos* like me. My slight physique encourages people. I hate dentists, merchants, lawyers, industrialists, civil servants, doctors, executives, the whole worthless bunch. All of them owe me, a lot. I opened my shirt, took out the .38, and asked with such rage that a drop of my spit hit his face, "What if I shove this up your ass?" He turned white, backed away. Pointing the revolver at his chest, I started feeling lighthearted: I took the drawers from the cabinets, dumped everything on the floor, kicked the vials as if they were balls. They crackled and exploded against the wall. Busting the cuspidor and motors was harder; I even hurt my hands and feet. The dentist looked at me. Several times he must have thought about jumping me; I hoped he would, so I could put a bullet in that big fat shit-filled belly of his.

"I'm not paying anything more, I'm tired of paying!" I shouted at him. "From now on I'm just taking!"

I shot him in the knee. I should've killed the sonofabitch.

The street full of people. I say, inside my head, and sometimes out loud, "Everybody owes me!" They owe me food, pussy, blankets, shoes, a house, car, watch, teeth, they owe me. A blind man is begging, rattling an aluminum cup with coins. I kick the cup, the sound of the coins irritates me. Marechal Floriano Street: gun store, pharmacy, bank, prostitute, portrait photographer. The electric company, vaccinations, doctor, clothing store, people everywhere. In the morning you can't even walk toward the train station, the crowd moves like some enormous lizard that takes up the entire sidewalk.

Those guys in Mercedes irritate me. The car's horn bugs me too. Last night I went to see a guy in Cruzada who had a Magnum with a silencer to sell, and when I was crossing the street some guy who'd been playing tennis in one of those fancy clubs blew his horn. I was distracted because I was thinking about the Magnum when the horn blew. I saw the car was moving slowly and stopped in front of it.

"What's your problem?" he shouted.

It was night and no one was around. He was wearing white. I took out the .38 and shot out his windshield, more to shatter the glass than to hit the guy. He gunned the car, to run me over or get out of there, or both. I jumped aside, and the car went by, its tires squealing on the asphalt. It stopped a few yards ahead. I went over. The guy was lying with his head back, his face and chest covered with thousands of tiny fragments of glass. He was bleeding from an ugly wound in his neck and his white clothing was all red.

He turned his head, which was leaning against the seat. His black eyes were bulging, and the whites were a milky blue. And because the whites of his eyes were bluish, I said, "You're dying, man. Want me to finish you off?"

"No, no," he said, strongly. "Please."

In the window of a building I saw a guy watching me. He hid when I looked at him. He must have called the police.

I walked away calmly, went back to Cruzada. It was great smashing the windshield of the Mercedes. I should've put a bullet in the hood and one in each door. Then the body shop guy would've had his work cut out for him.

The guy with the Magnum was already there. "Where's the dough? Put it in this sweet little hand," he said. His hand was white, smooth, but full of scars. My body is full of scars; even my dick is full of scars.

"I wanna buy a radio too," I told the smuggler.

While he went to get the radio, I examined the Magnum. Oiled and loaded. With the silencer it looked like a cannon.

The smuggler returned with a transistor radio. "It's Japanese," he said.

"Turn it on, so I can hear the sound."

He turned it on.

"Louder," I said.

He turned up the volume.

Poof. I think he died at the first shot. I shot twice more just to hear poof, poof.

They owe me high school. A girlfriend, sound equipment, respect, a mortadella sandwich at the lunch counter on Vieira Fazenda Street, ice cream, a soccer ball. I stay in front of the television to increase my hatred. When my rage is diminishing and I lose the desire to collect on what they owe me, I sit in front of the TV and my hatred comes back right away. I'd really like to get the guy who does one of the whiskey ads. He's all dressed up, nice looking, wrinkle-free, hugging a dazzling blonde and tossing ice cubes into a glass. He smiles, showing all his teeth, and his teeth are perfectly straight and real. I'd like to take a razor and slash both cheeks up to his ears, and those beautiful white teeth of his would be on the outside of a smiling red skull. He's there now, smiling, and he gives the blonde a kiss on the mouth. He can wait.

My arsenal is almost complete: I have the Magnum with the silencer, a Colt Cobra .38, two straight razors, a carbine 12, a snub-nosed Taurus .38, a dagger, and a machete. I'm going to cut off somebody's head with a single blow with the machete. I saw a ritual in the movies—in one of the Asian countries, back in the time of the English—that consisted of cutting off the head of an animal, a buffalo, I think, with a single blow. The English officers presided over the ceremony with an air of boredom, but the decapitators were true artists. One clean blow and the animal's head rolled, its blood gushing.

At the house of a woman who picked me up in the street. Middle-aged, says she goes to night school. I've been there, my school was the most nighttime of all the night schools in the world. It was so bad that it doesn't even exist anymore; it was demolished. Even the street it was on was demolished. She asks what I do, and I say I'm a poet, which is rigorously true. She asks me to recite a poem of mine. This: The rich like to go to sleep late / just because the rabble / have to go to sleep early to get to work in the morning / That's one more chance they / have to be different: / to parasitize, / to disdain those who work to earn their food, / to sleep late, / late / one day / good thing, / too much.

She cuts me off by asking if I like movies. "What about the poem?" She doesn't understand. I continue: I knew how to dance and fall in love / and roll on the floor / just for a time. / From the sweat of my brow nothing was built. / I wanted to die with her, / but that was another day, / yet another day. / In the Iris theater, on Carioca Street, / the Phantom of the Opera / A guy in black, / black briefcase, his face hidden, / in his hand an immaculate white handkerchief, / jerked off the spectators; / at the same time, in Copacabana, / another / who had not even a nickname, / drank the piss from the theaters' urinals / and his face was green and unforgettable. / History is made up of dead people / and the future of people who are going to die. / You think she's going to suffer? / She's strong, she will resist. / She would also resist if she were weak. / You, now, I don't know. / You pretended for so long, hit and screamed, deceived. / You're tired, / you're finished, / I don't know what keeps you alive.

She didn't understand anything about poetry. She was alone with me and tried to fake indifference, yawning in exasperation. The farcifying of women.

"I'm afraid of you," she finally confessed.

This poor, fucked-over woman doesn't owe me anything, I thought; she makes sacrifices to live in a two-room apartment, and her eyes have bags under them from drinking crap and reading about the life of society women in *Vogue*.

"Want me to kill you?" I asked as we drank cheap whiskey.

"I want you to fuck me," she laughed anxiously, in doubt.

Put an end to her? I had never strangled anybody with my bare hands. There's not much style, or drama, in strangling somebody; it looks like a street fight. Even so, I felt like strangling someone, but not a miserable person like her. For a nobody, only a bullet in the back of the head?

I've been thinking about that lately. She had taken off her clothes. Flat, wilted breasts, the nipples gigantic raisins that someone had stepped on. flaccid thighs with nodules of cellulite, spoiled gelatin with pieces of rotten fruit.

"I'm all shivery," she said.

I got on top of her. She grabbed me by the neck, her mouth and tongue in my mouth, a viscous vagina, hot and fragrant.

We fucked.

She's sleeping now.

I am just.

I read newspapers. The death of the smuggler in Cruzada wasn't even mentioned. The swell in the Mercedes died at the hospital, and the papers said he was attacked by a criminal from Boca Larga. What a laugh.

I write a poem called "Children or New Smells of Pussy": Here I am again / listening to the Beatles / on Mundial radio / at nine at night / in a room / that could belong / and did / to a mortified saint / There was no sin / and I don't know why they leper me / for being innocent / or stupid / In any case / the floor was always there / to dive into. / When you have no money / it's good to have muscles and hate.

I read the papers to find out what they are eating, drinking, and doing. I want to live a long life, so I have time to kill them all.

From the street I see the party on Vieira Souto, the women in long dresses, the men in black suits. I walk slowly, from one side of the sidewalk to the other; I don't want to awaken any suspicion—the machete inside my pants, strapped to my leg, doesn't allow me to walk right. I look like a cripple; I feel like a cripple. A middle-aged couple passes by and look at me with pity; I pity myself too. I limp and feel pain in my leg.

From the sidewalk I see the waiters serving French champagne. Those people like French champagne, French clothes, the French language.

I'd been there since nine o'clock, when I passed by, fully armed, at the whim of luck and misfortune, and the party had begun.

The parking places in front of the apartment were all occupied, and the guests started parking on the dark side streets. One of them, a red car with a young and elegant couple in it, interested me greatly. They walked to the apartment building without saying a word, with her adjusting her gown and hair and him his bow tie. They were preparing for a triumphal entrance, but from the sidewalk I saw that their entrance was, like the others', met with indifference. People get all beautified at the hairdresser, the designer, the masseur, and the only thing that gives them the attention they hope for at parties is a mirror. I saw the woman in her flowing blue dress and murmured, I'm going to give you the attention you deserve, it wasn't for nothing that you wore your best panties and made so many trips to the seamstress and rubbed all those creams on your skin and put on that expensive perfume.

They were the last to leave. They weren't walking with the same confidence, and they were irritated, arguing in slurred, confused voices.

I came up to them as the man was opening the car door. I was limping, and he gave me a quick, appraising glance and saw a low-rent, harmless cripple.

I stuck the revolver in his back.

"Do what I say or I'll kill you both," I said.

It wasn't easy getting in the back seat with my stiff leg. I had to stretch out, with the revolver pointed at his head. I told him to head for the Barra da Tijuca. I was pulling the machete out of my pants when he said, "Take the money and the car and leave us here." We were in front of the Hotel Nacional. What a laugh. He was sober by now and wanted to have another little whiskey while he phoned the police. Some people think life's a party. We drove toward the Recreio dos Bandeirantes, until we came to a deserted beach. We got out. I left the headlights on.

"We didn't do anything to you," he said.

They didn't? What a laugh. I felt hatred flooding my ears, my hands, my mouth, my entire body, the taste of vinegar and tears.

"She's pregnant," he said, pointing to the woman, "she's going to have our first child."

I looked at the belly of the slim woman and decided to be merciful. I said, "Poof," above where I judged her navel was, immediately wiping out the fetus. The woman fell face first. I placed the revolver against her temple and blew her brains out.

The man watched all this without a word, his wallet in his outstretched hand. I took the wallet from his hand, tossed it into the air, and, as it was falling, kicked it into the distance with my left foot.

I tied his hands behind his back with a rope I carried with me. Then I tied his feet.

"Kneel down," I said.

He kneeled.

The car's headlights lit his body. I kneeled beside him, removed his bow tie, and rolled his collar back, exposing his neck.

"Lower your head," I ordered.

He lowered it. I held the machete with both hands and raised it into the air. I saw the stars in the sky, the immense night, the infinite firmament, and brought the machete, the steel star, down with all my strength, right in the middle of his neck.

His head didn't fall off, and he tried to get up, thrashing about like a dizzy chicken in the hands of an incompetent cook. I struck him again and again and again and the head wouldn't come off. He had fainted, or died, with his goddamn head still on his neck. I threw the body over the car's fender. The neck was in a good position. I concentrated like an athlete who was about to do a somersault. This time, as the machete cut its mutilating path through the air, I knew I would get what I wanted. Plock! The head rolled along the sand. I raised the scimitar high and called: "Hail the Taker!" I gave a loud wordless cry. It was a long and powerful howl, so that all the animals would tremble and get out of my way. Where I walk, the asphalt melts.

A black toolbox under my arm. I say, stammering, that I'm the plumber here to do the work in apartment t-t-two-oh-one. The doorman thinks my stammering is funny and tells me to go on up. I start on the top floor. "I'm the plumber (not stammering now), I came to do the work." Through the opening, two eyes: nobody called the plumber. I go down to the seventh floor, the same thing. I only get lucky on the second floor.

The maid opened the door for me and shouted inside, "It's the plumber." A young woman in a nightgown appeared, a bottle of nail polish in her hand, pretty, maybe twenty-five.

"There must be some mistake," she said, "we don't need a plumber."

I took the Cobra from the toolbox. "Yes you do, and you better keep quiet or I'll kill both of you. Anybody else in the house?" Her husband was at work and the child at school. I tied up the maid and taped her mouth. I took the housewife into the bedroom.

"Take off your clothes."

"I'm not taking off my clothes," she said, head held high.

"They owe me cough syrup, socks, movies, filet mignon, and pussy. Move." I punched her in the head. She fell onto the bed, a red mark on her face. I don't shoot. I ripped off her nightgown, her panties. She wasn't wearing a bra. I opened her legs. I put my knees on her thighs. Her bush was thick and black. She stayed quiet, her eyes closed. It wasn't easy getting into that dark forest, her pussy was tight and dry. I bent over, opened the vagina and spit inside, spit copiously. Even so, it wasn't easy; I could feel my dick chafing. She groaned when I stuck my cock in as far as it would go. While I worked it back and forth, I licked her breasts, her ear, her neck, stuck my finger lightly into her ass, caressed her butt. My dick started to become lubricated by the juices of her vagina, which had become warm and viscous.

Because she wasn't afraid of me anymore, or because she *was* afraid of me, she came before I did. With the rest of the come from my dick I drew a circle around her navel.

"Don't open your door to the plumber again," I said as I was leaving.

I leave the house on Visconde de Maranguape. A large cavity in each molar full of wax from Dr. Lustosa / chew with the front teeth / jerk off to a magazine photo / stolen books.

I go to the beach.

Two women are talking on the sand. One has a suntanned body, a scarf on her head; the other is light-skinned—she must not come to the beach much. Both of them have very pretty bodies; the ass on the light-skinned one is the prettiest ass I've ever seen. I sit down nearby and look at them. They notice my interest and immediately start moving around, saying things with their bodies, making seductive movements with their fannies. At the beach we're all equal, us fucked-overs and them. We're better, even, because we don't have the big belly and flabby ass of the parasites. I want that white woman! And she's interested in me; she casts glances at me. They laugh and laugh, smiling. They say goodbye, and the white one heads toward Ipanema, the water wetting her feet. I get up and walk alongside her, not knowing what to say.

I'm a shy person, from having been beat up on all my life, and her hair is fine and well cared for, her neck is slender, her breasts small, her thighs are solid and round and muscular, and her ass is two hard hemispheres. A ballerina's body.

"Do you study ballet?"

"I used to," she says. She smiles at me. How can anyone have such a pretty mouth? I feel like licking it, tooth by tooth. "Do you live around here?" she asks. "Yes," I lie. She points to a beachfront building. It's all marble.

Back on Visconde de Maranguape Street. I'm killing time till I go to the white girl's house. Her name is Anna. I like palindromic Anna. I sharpen the machete on a special stone; that dandy's neck was very tough. The newspapers gave a lot of play to the couple I executed in the Barra. The woman was the daughter of one of those fuckers who get rich in Sergipe or Piauí by robbing peasants and then come to Rio. The children of those rednecks don't have an accent anymore, and they bleach their hair and claim they're descended from the Dutch.

The society columnists were flabbergasted. The jet-setters that I dispatched had tickets to Paris. No More Safety in the Streets, said the headline in one paper. What a laugh. I threw a pair of shorts into the air and tried to cut it with the machete, like Saladin used to do (with a silk handkerchief) in the movies.

They don't make scimitars like they once did / I am a hecatomb / It wasn't God or the Devil / who made me an avenger / It was I myself / I am the Penis-Man / I am the Taker.

I go into the room where Dona Clotilde has been bedridden for three years. Dona Clotilde owns the house.

"Want me to sweep the living room?" I ask.

"No, son, I just want you to give me an injection of B-12 before you leave."

I boil the syringe, prepare the injection. Dona Clotilde's butt is as dry as an old leaf and as wrinkled as rice paper.

"You're a gift from heaven, my son. You were sent here by God," she says.

There's nothing wrong with Dona Clotilde; she could get up and go shopping at the supermarket. Her illness is all in her head. And after three years in bed, only getting up to pee and crap, she probably doesn't have the strength.

One of these days I'll put a bullet in the back of her neck.

When I satisfy my hate I'm possessed by a sensation of victory, a euphoria that makes me feel like dancing—I give out small howls, grunts, inarticulate sounds that are closer to music than to poetry, and my feet glide along the ground, my body moves to a rhythm of sways and leaps, like a savage or a monkey.

Anybody who wants to order me around can try, but he'll die. I really would like to kill one of those big shots—with the paternal face of a successful crook—you see on television, a person whose blood is thick with caviar and champagne. Eat your caviar / your day is coming.

They owe me a toothy twenty-year-old girl with perfume. The girl in the marble building? I go in and she's waiting for me, sitting in the living room, quiet, unmoving, her hair very black, her face white, looking like a photograph.

"Let's go," I tell her. She asks me if I have a car. I tell her I don't own a car. She does. We take the service elevator down to the garage and get into a foreign convertible.

After a time I ask if I can drive and we trade positions. "Is

Petrópolis all right?" I ask. We climb the mountainside without a word; she's looking at me. When we get to Petrópolis she asks me to stop at a restaurant. I tell her I don't have any money and I'm not hungry, but she does and she is. She eats voraciously, as if they were going to snatch the plate away at any moment. A group of young people—junior executives, who drive up on Friday and have drinks before meeting their gussied-up wives to play cards or scarf down wine and cheese while they gossip about other people—are drinking and talking loudly at the next table. I hate executives. She finishes eating. "What now?" "Now we leave," I say, and we head back down the mountain, with me driving like lightning and her watching me. "My life has no meaning, I've thought about killing myself," she says. I stop on Visconde de Maranguape. "Is this where you live?" I get out without saying anything. She follows me. "Am I going to see you again?" I go in and hear the noise of the car pulling away as I climb the stairs.

Top Executive Club. You deserve the best in relaxation, with caring and understanding. Our masseuses do it all. Elegance and discretion.

I write down the address and go to the place, a house in Ipanema. I wait for him to appear, decked out in gray, vest, black briefcase, shoes shined, hair dyed. I take a piece of paper from my pocket, like someone looking for an address, and follow the guy to his car. These fuckers always lock their cars; they know the world is full of thieves, which they are too, except nobody ever catches them. As he unlocks the car I stick the revolver in his belly. Two men facing each other, talking, attract no attention. Sticking the gun in the back is scarier, but that should only be done in deserted spots.

"Keep quiet or I'll fill your executive belly with lead."

He has the petulant, and at the same time cheap, air of the ambitious man on the way up: come from the interior and dazzled by the society page, a shopper, right-wing voter, Catholic, religious seminar attendee, patriotic, comfort-loving, a sucker on the public teat, his kids studying at the Catholic university, his wife an interior decorator and partner in a boutique.

"So how was it, executive, did the masseuse jerk you off or suck your dick?"

"You're a man, you know how it is, you understand these things," he says. It's executive talk for the cab driver or elevator operator. From Podunk to the board room, he thinks he's already faced every kind of crisis situation.

"I'm not a goddamn man at all," I say softly, "I'm the Taker."

"I'm the Taker!" I shout.

He starts to turn the color of his clothes. He thinks I'm crazy, and he's never faced anyone crazy in his damned air-conditioned office.

"Let's go to your house," I say.

"I don't live here in Rio, I live in São Paulo," he says. He lost his courage but not his shrewdness. "What about the car?" I ask. "Car? What car? This car, with the Rio plates? I have a wife and three children," he says, changing the subject. What is this? An excuse, a password, habeas corpus, safe-conduct? I order him to stop the car. Poof, poof, poof, one shot for each child, in the chest. One in the head, for his wife, poof.

To forget the girl who lives in the marble building, I go to play soccer in the park. Three straight hours, my legs all banged up from the kicks I took, the big toe of my right foot swollen, maybe broken. Sweating, I sit down at the edge of the field, next to a black guy reading *O Dia*. The headline interests me; I ask to borrow the newspaper. The guy says, "You wanna read the paper why don't you buy one?" I don't get mad, the black guy only has two or three teeth, and they're dark and crooked. I say, "Right, let's not fight about it." I buy two hot dogs and a couple of cokes and give him half, and he gives me the paper. The headline says: Police Search for the Magnum Maniac. I hand the paper back to the guy. He doesn't accept it, and he laughs as he chews with his front teeth, or rather with his front gums, which are as sharp as razors from so much use. An item in the paper: A group of social-ites in the South Zone is frantically preparing for the traditional

Christmas dance, the First Cry of Carnival. The dance begins on December 24 and ends on the first day of the New Year; ranch owners from Argentina, heirs from Germany, American actors, and Japanese executives—the entire international parasite army—will be coming. Christmas has really turned into a party. Drink, frolic, orgy, idleness.

First Cry of Carnival. What a laugh. Those guys are funny.

Some nut jumped off the Rio-Niterói bridge and floated for twelve hours till a rescue launch found him. He didn't even catch a cold.

A fire in a nursing home killed forty old people; the families celebrated.

I just finished giving Dona Clotilde her injection of B-12 when the doorbell rings. The bell never rings at the house. I do the shopping, keep the place in order. Dona Clotilde has no relatives. I take a look from the balcony. It's Palindromic Anna.

We talk in the street. "Are you avoiding me?" she asks. "More or less," I say. We go into the house. "Dona Clotilde, there's a girl with me, can I take her up to my room?" "My boy, the house is yours, do whatever you want, I just want to see the girl."

We stand beside the bed. Dona Clotilde looks at Anna for a very long time. Her eyes fill with tears. "I've prayed every night," she sobs, "every night that you'll find a girl like this." She raises her arms, thin and covered with fine folds of skin, into the air, brings her hands together, and says, "Oh, my God, how I thank Thee."

We are standing in my room, eyebrow to eyebrow, like in the poem, and I take off her clothes and she takes off mine and her body is so beautiful that I feel a tightness in my throat, tears on my cheek, eyes burning, my hands tremble and now we're lying down, one on the other, entwined, moaning, and more, and more, without stopping, she screams, her mouth open, her teeth white like a young elephant's, "Oh, oh, I adore your obsession!" she shouts, water and salt and come spurt from our bodies, without end.

Now, much later, we lie there looking at each other, hypnotized, until nightfall, and our faces shine in the dark and the perfume of her body penetrates the walls of the room.

Anna awoke before I did, and the light is on. "You only have poetry books? And all these weapons, what for?" She gets the Magnum from the drawer, white flesh and black steel, and points it at me. I sit down on the bed.

"Want to shoot? You can shoot, the old woman isn't going to hear anything. A little higher." I raise the barrel to my forehead with the tip of my finger. "Here it doesn't hurt."

"Have you ever killed anyone?" Anna points the gun at my forehead.

"Yes."

"Was it good?"

"It was good."

"How so?"

"A relief."

"Like the two of us in bed?"

"No, no, something else. The other side of that."

"I'm not afraid of you," Anna says.

"Or me of you. I love you."

We talked until dawn. I feel a kind of fever. I make breakfast for Dona Clotilde and take it to her in bed. "I'm leaving with Anna," I tell her. "God has heard my prayers," the old woman says between swallows.

Today is December 24, the day of the Christmas dance or First Cry of Carnival. Palindromic Anna moved out and is living with me. Now my hatred is different. I have a mission. I always had a mission and didn't know it. Now I do. Anna helped me to see it. I know that if everyone who's fucked over did like me, the world would be better and more just. Anna taught me how to use explosives, and I think I'm now prepared for that change in scale. Killing one at a time is a mystical kind of thing, and I'm free of it. At the Christmas dance we'll kill as many as we can conventionally. It will be my final romantic, inconsequential gesture. We've chosen to initiate the new phase with the disgusting consumers at a supermarket in the South Zone. They'll be killed by a bomb. Goodbye, my machete, goodbye, my dagger, my rifle, my Colt Cobra, goodbye, my Magnum, today is the last time you'll be used. I kiss my machete. I'll blow up people, gain prestige; I won't be just the Magnum Maniac. And I also won't go to Flamengo Park to look at the trees, the trunks, the root, the leaves, the shade, choosing the tree I'd like to have, that I always wanted to have, on a piece of land with tamped earth. I saw them grow in the park and was happy when it rained and the ground got drenched with water, the leaves washed by rain, the wind ruffling the branches, while the bastards' cars sped by without them even looking to the side. I no longer waste my time on dreams.

"The whole world will know who you are, who we are," Anna says.

News item: The governor is going to come as Santa Claus. Item: Less festivity and more meditation, let's purify our hearts. Item: No shortage of beer. No shortage of turkey. Item: Christmas festivities this year will occasion more victims of traffic accidents and attacks than in previous years. Police and hospitals are gearing up for Christmas celebrations. The cardinal on television: the celebration of Christmas is warped, this is not its meaning, this business of Santa Claus is an unfortunate invention. The cardinal declares Santa Claus a fictitious clown.

"Christmas Eve is a good time for people to pay what they owe," Anna says. "I want to kill the Santa Claus at the dance with my machete," I say.

I read Anna what I sent to the newspapers, our Christmas manifesto. No more killing at random, without a definite objective. I didn't know what I wanted, didn't seek out a practical result, my hatred was being wasted. I was right in my impulses, my error was not knowing who the enemy was and why he was the enemy. Now I know; Anna taught me. And my example must be followed by others, many others. That's the only way we will change the world. That's the gist of our manifesto.

I put the weapons into a suitcase. Anna shoots as well as I do, she just doesn't know how to use the machete, but that weapon is obsolete now. We say goodbye to Dona Clotilde. We put the suitcase in the car. We go to the Christmas dance. There will be no shortage of beer, or turkey. Or blood. One cycle in my life ends and another begins.

BETSY

BETSY WAITED for the man to return to die.

Before the trip he had noticed that Betsy was unusually hungry. Then other symptoms emerged: excessive drinking of water, urinary incontinence. Betsy's only problem till then was the cataract in one of her eyes. She didn't like to go out, but before the trip she had unexpectedly come into the elevator with him and the two of them had strolled along the sidewalk by the beach, something she had never done.

The day the man arrived, Betsy had the hemorrhage and didn't eat. Twenty days without eating, lying on the bed with the man. The specialists he consulted said that there was nothing to be done. Betsy only left the bed to drink some water.

The man stayed in bed with Betsy throughout her agony, caressing her body, feeling sadness at the thinness of her hips. On the last day, Betsy, very quiet, her blue eyes open, stared at the man with the same gaze as ever, which indicated the comfort and pleasure produced by his presence and his affection. She began to tremble, and he hugged her more tightly. Feeling that her limbs were cold, the man arranged a comfortable position for Betsy on the bed. Then she extended her body, appearing to stretch, and turned her head away wearily. Then she stretched her body even more and sighed, a powerful exhalation. The man thought Betsy had died. But a few seconds later she emitted another sigh.

Horrified by his meticulous attention, the man counted each of Betsy's sighs one by one. She exhaled nine identical sighs, her tongue hanging outside her mouth. Then she began to beat her stomach with her legs, as she would occasionally do, only more violently. Immediately afterward, she became immobile. The man ran his hand lightly over Betsy's body. She stretched and extended her limbs for the last time. She was dead. Now, the man knew, she was dead.

The man spent the entire night awake at Betsy's side, lightly and silently caressing her, not knowing what to say. They had lived together for eighteen years.

In the morning, he left her on the bed and went to the kitchen to make coffee. He drank the coffee in the living room. The house had never been so empty and sad.

Fortunately, the man had not thrown out the cardboard box from the blender. He returned to the bedroom. He carefully placed Betsy's body in the box. With the box under his arm, he went to the door. Before opening it and going out, he wiped his eyes. He didn't want to be seen like that.

ANGELS OF THE MARQUEES

PAIVA CONTINUED to rise early, as he had done for the thirty years he worked unceasingly. He could have gone on working, but he had already made enough money and planned to travel with his wife Leila, to see the world while he still had his health and vigor. They purchased airline tickets a month after his retirement. But his wife died of a sudden illness before the trip, leaving Paiva alone and without plans for the future.

Paiva continued to rise early. He would read the newspaper and then go out, as he couldn't stay home with nothing to do. Besides which, the new maid was constantly bothering him, asking if she could throw out the old objects that had accumulated in the house, and making irritating noises as she straightened up; when he went into the kitchen, something he avoided doing, she would be accompanying some popular song on the radio, which was on throughout the day, in a tuneless voice. Also, he couldn't stand looking at the ocean anymore, that monotonous mass of water, the unchanging horizon that he saw from the balcony of his penthouse. Often he would leave the house without knowing where to go, and he would sit in Our Lady of Peace Square and watch the bands of parishioners coming out of the church. He wouldn't do that; he wouldn't start going to church now that he was old. He had never had any children with Leila, and he had discovered, too late, that he didn't have friends, just colleagues at work—he had no desire to see them now that he was retired. But what he missed was not companionship; he longed for an occupation, for something to do, perhaps to use his money to help others. He knew of guys who retired and were content to stay at home reading books and watching videotapes, or who spent their time taking their grandchildren to have ice cream or to Disney World, but he didn't like reading or seeing films; he'd never gotten used to that. Others joined philanthropic organizations and dedicated themselves to humanitarian works. He'd been invited to take part in an association that maintained an old people's home, but the visit to the home had left him very depressed. You have to be young to work with the old. There were also those retirees who couldn't take inactivity and died sick and unhappy. But he wasn't sick, only unhappy, and his health was quite good.

Whenever, just to get out of the house, he wandered aimlessly through the streets, Paiva would see people unconscious on the sidewalks. For many years he had gone from home to work in a chauffeur-driven car, and surely that scene had existed before without his ever noticing. He now knew, thanks to the suffering occasioned by his wife's death, that his selfishness had kept him from seeing the misfortune of others. It was as if fate, which had always protected him, were pointing out a new path, inviting him to help those wretches whom destiny had so cruelly abandoned. Some of them must be sick, others on drugs, while others, who were certainly hungry, had nowhere else to sleep and slept there. They didn't care about the passersby; shame is easily lost once a person has everything else taken away. There was no one as abandoned as some poor devil, filthy and wearing rags, unconscious in the gutter.

Once he was walking the streets, at nightfall, when he saw a man lying on the ground under the marquee of a bank. The homeless, whether unconscious or not, seemed to prefer bank marquees as their nocturnal refuge, perhaps because the bank managers did not, for some reason, feel at liberty to run them off. The passersby normally pretended to take no notice of an adult or child in this situation, but that night two people, a man and a woman, were deftly bending over an abandoned body, as if they were attempting to revive it. Paiva saw that they were trying to lift him from the ground, which they did skillfully, carrying him in their arms to a small ambulance. After the ambulance drove away, Paiva stood there for some time, thinking. Witnessing that gesture of charity had encouraged him: something, however modest, was being done; someone cared about those miserable creatures.

The next day, Paiva went out and walked the streets for a long time in search of the ambulance people. He wanted to offer to help in the work they did. He couldn't carry the wretched in his arms, for he had neither the inclination nor the skill of the selfless people he had seen that night, but he could, besides giving money, be useful in some administrative capacity. There must be a spot for someone with his experience in that group of volunteers, which he had named Angels of the Marquees, as it had been under a marquee that he had witnessed the gesture of solidarity. And every night he went out on his pilgrimage. He found several people fallen on the streets and had stood helplessly beside them, wishing for the Angels of the Marquees to appear.

Finally, one night, as he was heading home, discouraged, Paiva saw the pair of altruists lifting a body from the sidewalk and approached them. "I've been following your work and would like to help out," he said.

He received no reply, as if the Angels of the Marquees, absorbed in their task, had not heard him. A gray-haired man got out of the ambulance and helped the couple place the unconscious wretch onto a kind of stretcher inside the ambulance. Then the woman, who wore the glasses of a very nearsighted person, with her hair tied in a bun—she looked like a retired schoolteacher—asked what Paiva wanted.

He repeated that he would like to help in their work.

"How?" asked the woman.

"However you think best," Paiva said. "I have the time and I'm still pretty vigorous." He was going to add that he possessed financial resources, but thought it better to save that for later. "Please, I'd like to get your telephone number and address to visit you."

"Give us your phone number and we'll get in touch with you," said the gray-haired man, who appeared to be the leader of the group. "Write down his number, Dona Dulce."

"Do you belong to some social agency or health service connected to the government?"

"No, no," replied Dona Dulce, jotting down Paiva's telephone number, "we're a private organization. We want to keep people from dying abandoned in the streets."

"But we don't like publicity," said the gray-haired man. "Your right hand shouldn't know what your left hand is doing."

"That's how charity ought to be," said Dona Dulce.

Paiva waited anxiously for them to call, not leaving the house for a week. "They probably lost my number," he thought. "Or else they're so busy that they haven't had time to call." He consulted the telephone directory, but none of the charitable organizations he found was what he was looking for. He regretted not having paid more attention to the ambulance, which must have had some identifying marks that could have helped him now. Maybe it was better to look for it in the streets. He knew that the Angels of the Marquees did their emergency medical work at night, so Paiva went back to roaming the streets every night, waiting for the Angels to appear under one of the marquees, next to the fallen bodies. One night, during yet another of his walks, he saw an ambulance in the distance. It was stopped at the curb. He ran toward it, and there were the Angels of the Marquees, bent over the motionless body of a young man.

"You didn't call me, I looked in the phone book, I didn't know how to find you—"

The Angels of the Marquees appeared surprised at Paiva's presence.

"Dona Dulce," Paiva said, "I almost ran an ad in the paper looking for you."

Dona Dulce smiled.

"I live by myself; my wife died, I have no relatives, so I'm completely available to work with you. You'd be like a new family to me."

Dona Dulce smiled again, fixing her hair; the bun had come undone.

The gray-haired man got out of the ambulance and asked, "Did you lose his address, Dona Dulce?"

The woman remained silent for a time, as if she didn't know what to say. "Yes, I did," she answered finally.

"Let me take it down again." The man wrote Paiva's name and phone number on a pad. "We don't like publicity," he said apologetically.

"I know, the right hand shouldn't know what the left hand is doing," Paiva said.

"That's our philosophy," said the man. "You can rest assured that I'll take care of getting in touch with you myself."

"Is that a promise?"

"Just stay home and wait; I'll call you soon. The more people helping out, the better for us. My name is José," he said, holding out his hand in greeting.

The next day, Paiva received the long-awaited phone call. With pleasure he recognized the voice of Dona Dulce, who said that he had been accepted to work with the group. They were in need of people like him to work with them, and they were in a hurry. Could Paiva meet them that night at the same place? "Under the marquee?" Paiva replied. Yes, under the marquee, Dona Dulce confirmed, at the same hour. "There's no better place than that to meet with the Angels of the Marquees," Paiva said. But the voice at the other end did not respond to his comment.

Paiva arrived early, as soon as night had descended on the city, and waited for the ambulance. Only José was in it.

"You don't know how happy I am with your decision," said Paiva, approaching the ambulance and verifying that it had no identifying words or numbers on it.

"Get in, please," said José, who was at the wheel. Paiva opened the door and sat down beside him. "I'm taking you to our head-quarters, so you can get to know our work better," said José.

"Thank you very much." Paiva said, "I don't know how to repay you for what you're doing for me. My life was very empty."

José drove fast, but that must be how you drive an ambulance. At one point José took out a pack of cigarettes and asked if the smoke would bother him. Paiva told him no, he could smoke as much as he liked. With the exception of that brief exchange, the trip was carried out in silence. Finally, they arrived at their des-tination. The gates were opened, and the ambulance went in and stopped in the courtyard, where, in addition to the cars, there was a motorcycle with large side bags. Nearby, a rider in a black jacket, gloves, and helmet, the visor covering his eyes, paced back and forth impatiently. "The director should be along shortly. In the meantime, I'll show you our facilities," José said as they got out of the car. "Let's start with the infirmary."

Paiva walked down the corridor, accompanied now by two orderlies. When they arrived at the small infirmary, he was im-pressed at the cleanliness of the place, just as he had already ad-mired the immaculate whiteness of the orderlies' uniforms. This was the first time he had felt totally happy since his wife died. At that moment the orderlies immobilized him, tied his hands, and placed him on a stretcher. Surprised and frightened, Paiva could offer no resistance. A needle was stuck into his arm. "What—" he managed to say, but he didn't finish the sentence.

They removed his clothing and took him to a bathroom on the stretcher. His body was washed and sterilized, and he was immediately taken to an operating room, where two men in aprons, gloves, and surgical masks were waiting. He was put on the operating table and quickly anesthetized. Blood was taken from his arm and rushed to the laboratory beside the room by an orderly.

"What can we use from this one?" asked one of the men in masks, his voice muffled by the cloth covering his mouth.

"The corneas, for sure," replied the other, "then we'll check whether the liver, kidneys, and lungs are in good shape; you never know."

The corneas were removed and placed in a receptacle. Then Paiva's body was sliced up. "We have to work fast," one of the men in masks said, "the rider's waiting to deliver the orders."

THE ENEMY

1.

I do a lot of thinking, which always happens before I lie down, when I lock the doors to the house. That gets me extremely irritated because when I go back to bed, despite the mnemonic exercises I use to be sure I've locked the doors and windows, doubt assails me and I have to get up again. There are nights when I get up five, six, seven times, until finally, all uncertainty dissipated, I go to sleep with my mind at ease. Tonight, for example, I've already gotten up twice, to see if the doors were really locked, but I'm still not sure. The mnemonic exercises I was using seemed to be good ones. At the window to the balcony I spat between the blinds and saw, as I shut the latch, a drop of saliva quivering and reflecting the light from the streetlamp. At the front door, as I locked the bolt, I exclaimed *alea jacta est* twice. After locking the back door I lifted my leg and touched the knob with the sole of my foot. It was cold. Then I lay down, hoping to return calmly to Ulpiniano the Gentle, Mangonga, Najuba, Felix, Roberto, and Myself. At that instant, in bed, the word *return* made me realize, in distress, that in making my security rounds I wasn't concentrating on those essential tasks (thieves had twice entered my house and stolen a substantial part of my belongings), but rather thinking distractedly, which couldn't give me the certainty of having done my routine with precision. In fact, when I locked the door and exclaimed *alea jacta est,* I was thinking about the monkey that spoke to Vespasiano, father of Ulpiniano the Gentle and Justin, his brother and a magician by profession, to whom I was helper. Despite some people saying I was a magician's assistant out of dilettantism, in reality what interested me was the money I made at each show, which helped pay for my studies, as I wasn't all that crazy about the job itself, especially because of the fact that Justin demanded I work in a bow tie. We performed our show in circuses and clubs. The circuses were almost always in the outskirts and on Saturday and Sunday; besides the nighttime show (nine o'clock), there was a matinee (four o'clock). That meant I would spend practically all day Saturday and Sunday outside the city and there was no point in going home. That didn't bother me, as I was going out with (but she didn't know it) Aspásia, the girl from Peru, or Ecuador, maybe Bolivia, the trapeze artist. She would climb up (in a short red satin skirt and holding a colorful parasol, how pretty she was), her face tense, her body made of balance and power, and slide lightly and deftly on the steel wire. But she didn't want anything to do with me because I was only fifteen years old and was nothing.

It's necessary to put some order to the events. We're at the high school, and I'm a student and magician's helper. It's Monday; I'm sad because on Sunday I went to Aspásia and recited "La Casada Infiel" for her, in Spanish, and after listening smilingly (to what I thought would move her to tears), she ended the matter by saying that my Spanish was disgusting. Not in those words, but that was the idea. I had to go to school, when what I wanted was to be on the island of Cayo Icacos, which I had discovered in the atlas and which must have coconut palms, blue sea, and cool breezes, with Aspásia at my side.

The first class was with House Wren, so nicknamed because he was skinny and his arms looked like the wings of some ugly bird. We hated him: young people don't forgive the weak. Mangonga was reading a sex book, "Deluxe Courtesans," in the back row.

Ulpiniano the Gentle appeared to be paying attention to the class, but I knew that was impossible; Felix was taking notes; Najuba was taking notes; and Roberto, his eyes turned away, was telling lies. We no longer enjoyed ridiculing House Wren, who, because he was deaf, allowed the ridicule to go on without great risk. That day, after the class, Roberto called me and said, "Look, I'm going to tell you something that I don't have the courage to tell anyone, not my mother, not my father, not my brothers," which was no big deal because Roberto was a guy who lived isolated at home, reading treatises on parapsychology, without any possibility of communication with his parents, who had had him late in life. He was at least twenty years younger than his brothers. His face was like this: pale, with rings under his eyes (he spent the nights reading, hidden from his mother), and he had a very long nose, even for a grown man. So it was no big deal for him to tell me what he-hadn't-even-told-his-mother, etc. He pulled me aside and spoke only when, despite being alone in the corner of the hallway, he was sure no one could hear us.

"I flew today," he said. His eyes gleamed.

"You did?" I said. I didn't know if I believed or not. Not him, the flying. He never lied.

"I flew. I swear it. You believe me, don't you?" he said, looking at me anxiously. "I rose twenty centimeters off the ground."

We went to the bar on Vieira Fazenda street. We ordered coffee with milk and a bologna sandwich, a splurge. He told me the details of how the thing had happened, which was more or less like this: it was right after he'd finished reading a book by Sir W. Crooks, *Researches in the Phenomena of Spiritualism*. When Crooks wrote the book, in 1920, no one accepted such things except the believers. (And even so, St. Teresa and St. John of the Cross, who were seen suspended in the air, are known for other talents and not those. St. Joseph of Copertino, despite having flown more than 100 times, never achieved any great prestige in religious history because he was kind of a dim-bulb saint.) Outside the religious field, parapsychological phenomena, like telepathy, clairvoyance, and other forms of extrasensory perception, weren't

much believed in. Roberto had begun with experiments related
to ESP by reading Murchison, Rhine, Sval, Goldney, Bateman,
and Zorab. Then Richet, Osty, Saltmarsh, Johnson, and Pratt.
As well as Schmeidler, McConnell, Myers, and Podmore. And
finally, Schrenk-Notzing, Playne, and L. S. Bendit. There wasn't
anybody who'd read more about parapsychology than him. He
corresponded with the Psychical Society of England. He wrote to
S. P. Bogvouvala, in India, and together they did wonders (one
read the other's thoughts at a distance). But to Roberto being a
medium, hypnotizer, and telepath were minor things. His true
interest was levitation. "It's all a matter of controlling the body's
energies," he said. He wasn't a mystic, a condition that perhaps
made things easier. (See H. H. C. Thruston, *The Physical Phenomena of Mysticism*.) But he had strong will power. One day, that
day, he began concentrating in the morning; his family was away,
it was a weekend, and he'd stayed behind to study for his exams.
He didn't have lunch, and he didn't eat anything during the day,
or have dinner. He felt an enormous power gathering within
him; it was gaining strength and momentum. Night came. As day
began to break, he saw that his body was starting to lift itself off
the floor; he remained in the air for some time, a long time, until
he felt the power leaving him and he came back down.

2.

Can Roberto still fly today? That's something I need to clarify.
But not just that. And what about the resurrection of Ulpiniano
the Gentle? And the talking monkey?

Obviously I didn't believe, at the time, in the talking monkey.
Vespasiano, the father of Ulpiniano the Gentle and Justin, whose
profession was Magic, claimed to carry on intelligent conversations with the monkey. The two of them really did talk all the
time, when Vespasiano wasn't out getting into movies for free.
Vespasiano never missed the premiere of a new film, but he always
snuck in; to him it was a matter of honor, of etiquette, to get into
the theater without paying. It was relatively easy for him. He was
an enormous man who dressed in conspicuous and irresistible

fashion: spats, dark clothing, vest, a flower in his lapel, cane, and homburg. Despite his strange appearance, the outfit served his purpose, which was to get into the theater for free. His technique was simple. He would start to go in, solemnly; without stopping at the door, he would greet the attendant and head straight for the projection room. In 99 percent of the cases the attendant didn't have the courage to ask for his ticket. It was impossible to resist Vespasiano's overwhelming presence. Sometimes a distracted (or crazy) doorman would ask for his ticket. Vespasiano would crush him by saying, "What do you mean? Don't you know who I am?" Even the toughest attendant would meekly give in.

But his favorite pastime was talking with the monkey. It wasn't unusual to see Vespasiano conversing with the monkey. One day I went to see Ulpiniano the Gentle and neither he nor Vespasiano was at home. Justin was practicing *legère-de-main* by making a coin travel across the back of his hand: finger-knuckle-finger, back and forth; then he got a ping-pong ball, then a deck of cards. That was how he relaxed, by training his fingers, making his hand faster than the eye. I went straight to the room where the monkey was. We were vis-à-vis, alone. I slapped him, and he fell off the table where he was sitting. I left him lying on the floor and went to watch Justin and his sleight-of-hand training while I waited for Vespasiano to arrive, when we would get to the bottom of this business of the talking monkey.

Vespasiano arrived, portentous, filling the place with energy. Immediately the monkey, silent till then, began to shriek. Vespasiano ran to him.

"Yes, yes?"

"Keen-keen, keen-keen, kee."

"Really?"

"Keen-kee-kee-kee."

"Frightful! Infamous! Vile!"

Vespasiano was in the habit of speaking in adjectives. He had read Rui Barbosa and had never recovered.

"Ha!"

That *ha* sounded like the roar of a lion, and he turned and came toward me. I waited for him, paralyzed with fear: he really did talk to the monkey! Controlling himself, he asked me:

"Why did you commit such a savage act against him? He never hurt anyone. He's most noble and courageous of animals, among men and beasts, that I have met. A slap in the face, unexpected, unjust, cruel, petty, and impertinent. Explain yourself."

I apologized to the monkey.

It was more or less in that period that Ulpiniano the Gentle was expelled from school. He had already been suspended after a hygiene test; instead of answering the questions, he wrote slogans like "drink more milk" and "sleep with the windows open" (adding "signed: the burglar"), and he wrote an essay, "Menopause in Fowls." When called in by the headmaster, Ulpiniano the Gentle replied that the essay, despite being impertinent, was a scientific contribution to aviculture, and he asked the head to hear the opinion of Dr. Karl Bisch, the leading specialist on the subject, who would surely attest to the importance of his work.

They didn't ask Dr. Karl Bisch's opinion, and Ulpiniano the Gentle was suspended. In any case, it would have been difficult to get Dr. Karl Bisch's opinion for the simple reason that he didn't exist. He was one of the characters Ulpiniano the Gentle, Roberto, Mangonga, and I had invented to make fun of our teachers. Whenever possible, we would cite nonexistent authors on tests, trusting in the traditional ignorance of our teachers. Of course we sometimes took chances, like the time on the literature test that I cited Sparafucile as "the well known Italian critic of Veda literature," or when Mangonga cited his own father, whose name was Epifânio Catolé, as "an eminent Bahian historian." Mangonga's case was a little different from ours—he believed the lies he told, and after the test he began saying that his father didn't get the recognition he deserved because he was averse to publicity.

Mangonga said he lived in Copacabana. In those days Copacabana wasn't yet the slum with the highest population density in the world; it was a place where elegant, rich people lived. Every day after school Mangonga and Najuba would go to Copacabana together, and Najuba, who lived on Miguel Lemos, would get out before Mangonga, who lived on Avenida Atlântica, in Posto 6. Mangonga did that for four years, until one day his father died and we went to his house for the wake. Mangonga's place was on Cancela Street, in São Cristóvão, on the second floor of an old two-story house with a rotting, creaky staircase and a broken handrail. There was no beach and no ocean, no girls in bathing suits. The afternoon sun was blazing, and the heat was so strong and oppressive that even the cadaver of Mangonga's father was sweating.

After that, of course, Mangonga never went home with Najuba again. His father's death made him become even more interested in questions of demonology. Roberto said Mangonga was "the only mythomaniac who had a pact with the devil." But his main concern was with vampires and succubi, female demons who take advantage of sleeping people to commit all kinds of evil.

Getting back to Ulpiniano the Gentle's expulsion, one day when I got to school I saw a lot of students gathered in front of the bulletin board. Must be a very important notice, I thought. And so it was. A large poster, painted in red and blue letters, read:

FATHER JÚLIO MARIA & CO. ANNOUNCE TO THEIR
DISTINGUISHED CLIENTELE THEIR NEW PRICE LIST

1. COMMUNIONS	
SIMPLE HOSTS	1.00
HEART OF PALM HOSTS	2.00
SHRIMP-FILLED HOSTS	8.00
GILDED HOSTS WITH EFFIGY OF THE POPE (NOT BE TO SWALLOWED)	500.00
2. BAPTISMS	
WITH PLAIN WATER	10.00
WITH SALTED MINERAL WATER	30.00
WITH GENUINE VICHY WATER AND IMPORTED SODIUM CHLORIDE	80.00

3. MARRIAGES	
SIMPLE	30.00
WITH FLOWERS AND SOME CANDLES	100.00
WITH A FEW MORE FLOWERS, LIGHTS, ORGAN, AND AMATEUR SINGER	400.00
WITH ROSES, ORGAN, CARPET, PRIEST IN NEW CLOTHES, LIGHTS, AND PROFESSIONAL SINGER	1,000.00
WITH DUTCH TULIPS, PROFUSE LIGHTING, RED CARPET, BISHOP IN NEW CLOTHES, SOCIETY-PAGE PHOTOGRAPHER, ORGAN, AND PROFESSIONAL CELESTIAL CHOIR (WITH RECORDED MUSIC)	40,000.00
4. EXTREME UNCTIONS	
SOULS WITHOUT SIN, COMMENDED BY DAY	10.00
SOULS WITHOUT SIN, COMMENDED BY NIGHT, UP TO 10 P.M.	20.00
SOULS DITTO, COMMENDED AFTER 10 P.M.	80.00
SOULS WITH MORTAL SINS (DAY OR NIGHT)	100.00
5. BLESSINGS	
BLESSING WITH SAINT OF WOOD OR ALUMINUM	6.00
BLESSING WITH SAINT OF SILVER, GOLD, OR PRECIOUS STONES	40.00
BLESSING OF RESIDENCE OF UP TO TWO BEDROOMS, LIVING ROOM, BATHROOM, KITCHEN, AND MAID'S QUARTERS	95.00
BLESSING OF RESIDENCE WITH SWIMMING POOL OR BILLIARDS ROOM	600.00

OUR PRICES ARE THE LOWEST IN TOWN.
NO COMPETITORS.
WE SUPPLY PRIESTS TO GIVE YOUR PARTIES A PIOUS TOUCH.
SAINTS, PAPAL BULLS, IMAGES, ORATORIOS,
RELIGIOUS BOOKS, SPLINTERS FROM THE CROSS.
ALL FOR THE LOWEST PRICE. COME SEE US.

–JÚLIO MARIA & CO.

That was what was written. The Headmaster thought Ulpiniano the Gentle was crazy and expelled him from the school. Ulpiniano the Gentle went home and died, in order, as he said, to be resurrected at the end of the seventh day, "just like Jesus Christ." He had always liked Jesus Christ. He would say, quoting Fernando Pessoa, "better was Jesus Christ, who didn't understand finance and it's uncertain whether he had a library."

He was at home when he died. We were in the living room and he said, "I'm going to die, just like Jesus Christ."

He lay down on the floor and, uh, died. His body became rigid and he began to expire. Najuba and I didn't believe it at first, and since it was all a joke, we started kidding around. First we wrote JESUS CHRIST on his forehead, and we placed, or rather Najuba placed, because he was the one who read Pitigrilli, a poster on Ulpiniano the Gentle's chest with YNRJ in huge letters and in parentheses in smaller letters: I'M BATTY. Then, using various rubber stamps we found around the house, we stamped his arms and cheeks: "Approved," "Filed," "Personal," "Confidential," "Non-Transferable."

Right after Ulpiniano the Gentle disappeared, school started to be a drag. Roberto didn't fly anymore. None of our plans succeeded. The day Mangonga suggested going to the District was a total failure. Before we got there Najuba backed out. "Just pop into the bar first and take off the weight," Mangonga said. "It's not 'cause of that, I don't have the weight on today, it's just that I've got something important to do," Najuba replied. I said, "The reason may not be the weight, but I know you're wearing the weight. You without the weight is like Felix without the clothespin." This was something that Felix didn't like to hear, and he immediately said he wasn't going either because he had something important to do. "Okay, so I'm wearing the weight," Najuba said. "Then take it off, go into the bar's bathroom and take it off." "But that's not it," Najuba said, "I don't want to go." Mangonga said, "You're scared, you chicken-shit. What good did it do to have that lead weight tied to your dong all these years, huh? It didn't grow, did it? Didn't I say it wouldn't grow?" "It grew," Najuba said. Mangonga: "How much? How much? A quarter inch? Half an inch? Like hell it grew!"

Mangonga and I were by ourselves. Little by little we started getting skittish too. "What if we catch a disease?" I asked. I thought about Aspásia; I wanted to do that thing with Aspásia. "Disease?" Mangonga asked. "What disease?" "Gonorrhea, chancres, buboes, whatever." We shuddered just thinking about the stories of syphilitic guys getting gonorrhea of the groin. We ended up at the Primor theater, sucking on jawbreakers and watching serials. When we left, I stopped at a hardware store and bought a huge clothespin to give Felix as a present. Felix slept with a clothespin on his nose every night, to narrow it. He thanked me, with tears in his eyes, when he saw the strong spring and the width of the clothespin. "You guys treated Najuba real badly," he said. He was the only one who understood Najuba. "Don't you think my nose is narrower?" he asked me.

SECOND PERIOD

3.

I'm still in bed, and all of this was memory at work. Or was it? Today I'm a man filled with doubts. I don't really know if I locked the doors, and that's preventing me from falling asleep; I even feel a weight on my chest. I need to sleep. Let's see: when I locked the door to the balcony I went toc-toc with my tongue against my lips. At the front door I spotted the number nine on the bolt of the lock and touched my nose to the knob. It was cold. When I got to the back door I said, *Hattie, Henry, and the Honorable Harold hold hands together in Hampstead Heath,* practicing, as I applied the mnemonic trick, the aspirated *h* in my English. But even so, I remain in doubt. It was because I didn't for a moment stop thinking, "What if those things were real?" Such stupid things, but I don't know if they were real. Could they be dreams? But whoever dreams also sleeps. The guy dreams in order to sleep. There's no sleep without dreams. How I wish I could sleep. I'm going—no, no. What I've always wanted to know is whether the people, and the facts, are real. I don't care about knowing if the people exist or no longer exist, if the facts exist or don't exist. It was because of this that, many years later, I tried to find out the Truth. I testify with satisfaction that, despite being in distress, I don't lose my lucidity for a moment; the search I carried out was tiring and perhaps futile, but, even so, I do not give in to despair and manage to be more or less droll.

The search. First, however, are the doors locked? I'm not afraid that the burglar will catch me awake: there the advantage is all mine. But sleeping? Ha, that's silly, my doubts won't let me sleep. A doubtful man never sleeps.

How long afterward was it that I began my search? I think it was twenty years later, let's see, that's right, twenty years later, like in Dumas's novel. How? I'm starting to get confused, not exactly confused, it's that thing that happens. Shit, I don't know anything anymore. At this moment I'd like to be on the sea, in a boat with an enormous white sail, far away.

I went twenty years without seeing those guys. The idea that I needed to see them again wouldn't leave my mind. Why? I didn't know for sure. It was a kind of obsession that gripped me night and day, nevertheless I put off initiating everything—a simple call to Roberto, after consulting the phone book—for years.

"Who?" he said at the other end of the line.

I repeated my name. "From high school, don't you remember?" I said my name again.

"Ah! Yes, yes. So many years . . . How are you?"

"Fine. I'd like to see you."

"Of course, one of these days."

"Tomorrow? How about lunch?"

"Tomorrow I can't. I don't think I can. I may have to go to São Paulo. For two or three days."

"How about Friday?"

"Friday? I don't know. Here at home it's hard to give an answer. Could you call my office and set up a time with my secretary? She's the one who knows my schedule. Is that okay?"

We met two weeks later. He had become a very busy man. "I

arranged half an hour for you," his secretary had said, with the air of someone who'd done me a great favor.

Roberto no longer had dark circles under his eyes. His nose was still very long, he had put on weight, and there was a great deal of gray in his hair. His face was lined with wrinkles and he appeared to be the kind of man who was in a continual state of exhaustion.

ROBERTO: Is there anything I can do for you?

ME: What? No. I just came for a chat. Nostalgia for the old days.

ROBERTO: (*Looking at his watch*) Hmm. I know. I know.

ME: Do you still remember the old days?

ROBERTO: I'm consumed by the present. I'm an executive, I have to make decisions. I can't think about the past; I barely have time to think about the future.

SECRETARY: Mr. Roberto, a phone call from São Paulo.

ROBERTO: Excuse me. (*Picks up the telephone*) Hello? Yes. Yes. No. Yes. Yes. No. No, absolutely not. Yes. Yes. No, not in any fashion. (*Hangs up*) Imbeciles.

ME: Do you remember Ulpiniano the Gentle?

ROBERTO: Ulpiniano?

ME: Yes, that guy who played football with us, in jacket and tie. Remember?

ROBERTO: I didn't play football.

ME: You didn't play football? How can that be? You mean you never got in those pickup games with us?

ROBERTO: No. I never played sports. You must be confusing me with someone else.

ME: Hey, that's right. Now I remember. You didn't like sports, you liked to read, that's all you did, read.

(*The secretary comes in*)

SECRETARY: The list of people who'll be at the 11:45 meeting. (*She places a sheet of paper on Roberto's desk*)

ME: That's it exactly, you didn't like football.

ROBERTO: (*Reading the paper*) Precisely.

ME: That's its exactly. Ulpiniano the Gentle didn't like it either, he just played to round out the team. He didn't like spoiling any-body's fun. "Treat everyone with kindness and understand-ing," that was his motto. That's why he chose the surname "the Gentle." He *was* gentle. Do you remember him?

ROBERTO: (*Checking his watch*) I remember he didn't go to the barber very often.

ME: You remember the day he died?

ROBERTO: Did he die?

ME: Right after that business with Father Júlio Maria & Co.

ROBERTO: Father Júlio Maria & Co.?

ME: And what about your flying?

ROBERTO: My flying?

ME: Yes, your flying? You flew. Eight inches off the ground.

(*The secretary comes in*)

SECRETARY: They're waiting for you in the meeting room.

Roberto doesn't answer. The secretary sees that he hadn't heard and repeats uneasily: "They're waiting for you in the meet-ing room." Roberto gets up. He nods at me and silently leaves the room.

4.

Why is it I never married? Getting married is an act of normal-ity. Everybody gets married, except, of course, for homosexuals, women who don't find husbands, self-indulgent egotists, rebels. However, I'm not any of those, and I didn't get married. Maybe because I never met a woman I cared about, or rather, a woman I cared about who also cared about me. I only really cared about Aspásia, starting when I was fifteen, in the days when I assisted Justin the Magician. After I stopped working in the circus, I saw Aspásia only once more, five years later. I didn't yield my strength, as Alain said, or would say, to any woman during those five years. After Aspásia rebuffed the first proposal I made to her, I stopped working as a magician's assistant and decided to change my life. She said, "Come back when you grow up." She humiliated me, laughed at me—I discovered that day that she had a gold tooth in her mouth. I never saw a body like hers, in the circus, at the beach, at the Municipal Theater dances, in the movies, in photo magazines. She was the same color all over. Under the arms, the neck, the belly, the knees, all the color of old roof tile. Her flesh clung to the bone, made of muscle that didn't show. Her buttocks and the part of her thighs beneath the buttocks were firm—it's there that you have to look at a woman's body. No other place can better indicate the resistance and future of the flesh, how its form and its texture is, or will be, in the adult woman.

5.

Felix received me with a glass in his hand, his arms spread, smiling, protective. Especially smiling. "Want a whiskey?" he asked, "The good stuff? How do you like that Gobelin?" He was a happy man, one of the self-satisfied kind who aren't bashful about aggressively demonstrating their happiness, even to men in distress.

He insisted on calling his wife. In the meantime I looked around the living room: bookcases on the walls, leather-bound books, colorful collections laid out symmetrically, complete works.

The woman was a pale blonde, and she had disguised a pimple on her forehead with makeup. The children were also blond, but a darker, suspect blond.

They showed themselves and disappeared.

"That mirror's over two hundred years old."

"It looks like a Jean Baptiste Poquelin original. Is it?"

"I don't know. I think so. Now I remember, my father-in-law said it was."

But that brought me no joy. Something like that should have been said to Ulpiniano the Gentle, and whether he fell for it or not, I would amuse myself the same way. Nor did it make me feel pity.

Felix told me he had a full life: professors Such-and-Such were giving him private lessons in economics, sociology, the history of art, and philosophy.

"A man in my position has to constantly refine himself, sharpen his intelligence, keep up with the times."

The cretin. He had an enormous smile on his face. He was fat, and he was sweating.

"And you, how are you?" he asked, looking me up and down. Then: "I'm going to give you some advice—your shirt collar is too open, they don't wear it like that anymore. The collar is directly in the field of vision of the person you're talking to; after the teeth it's the first thing you see. It has to be irreproachable."

"What about the nose?"

"The nose?"

"The nose. Does the one being talked to see the other's nose as much as his teeth and collar?"

He thought for a moment.

"Less."

"Speaking of noses: do you still use the clothespin?"

"What clothespin?"

"The clothespin you used to put on your nose every night before you went to sleep. I never asked you, but I think you used it to narrow your nose. Was it really to narrow your nose or was it some kind of superstition?"

"I don't know what you're talking about."

"Look, Felix, I once gave you a clothespin so wide and strong that you cried with gratitude. It was the day that we'd gone to the District with Mangonga and Najuba."

"You're crazy. Why would I use a clothespin on my nose?" He attempted a guffaw.

"To narrow it."

The conversation stopped there. He was annoyed. I didn't want to argue with him. There was a lot I wanted to find out.

"Are you annoyed, Felix?" That was an opening for me to apologize. But he didn't understand.

"Nothing irritates me as much as rudeness in people."

"Really."

"With some people you can't, and shouldn't, have any meaningful intimacy."

"How so?"

"Men of breeding must have friends with breeding."

"Really."

But his anger didn't go away.

"My father always said: you shouldn't invite just anyone into your home."

The cretin. His lips were thicker, and everything about him was more mulatto: his hair all wavy, his nostrils like a couple of flaccid hazelnuts, his gums purple.

I tried. I began, "You remember that day."

"I don't remember anything. I think you'd better leave."

"What? You're ordering me out?"

He stood up.

"You imbecile," I said, "just because you married rich, to a blonde, inherited a Gobelin from your father-in-law, take lessons in the history of philosophy from some asshole professor, just because of that, you cretin, you think you're really something. Idiot. I don't know what's stopping me from rearranging your face."

"You're in my house," he stammered, feigning toughness.

I left. In the hall I noticed a boy looking at the two of us. At the time I thought nothing of it and slammed the outside door loudly, but at home I thought about the boy, witnessing the humiliation of his father.

6.

I said I loved only Aspásia, but that's not true; when I think about Aspásia I think I loved only her, but when I think about the other one I know it's not true. There was another girl: I fell in love with her before I saw the whites of her eyes. I remained at a distance, looking at her, while from her window she was looking at something that must have been the sea. From where I was, I could see the balcony, the dining room, and the bedroom. He would come to see her twice a week. On those days she would put on some makeup, sit in the living room and wait; then, when I least expected it, he would appear, sometimes just after nightfall, other times quite late, when I would already be tired of waiting. He would insert the key in the lock, go into the living room, without kissing or greeting her, take off his coat and place it over the back of a chair, and go to the bedroom.

The next day she would take a long time to appear on the balcony; when she came out I would concentrate and say, softly, "Look this way, my love, look this way," and stare at her without blinking, until my eyes burned. She never saw me, never looked at me. I bought a parrot and took it to my balcony, to see if she'd look my way, but the parrot wouldn't say a word and she went on looking at the ocean. I bought a horn. When she appeared I blew the horn for all I was worth, but not the faintest sound came out. I blew, blew, blew till I was dizzy. I had no strength; I hadn't eaten for two days: I had a couple of egg yolks, ate a baguette with butter, a can of sausages, and six bananas and went back to the balcony with the horn and blew. I blew without managing any sound at all, till I became nauseous and vomited everything. Lying in bed, with the acid taste of vomit still in my mouth, I thought: she must be blind, that's why she doesn't see me; the only thing I have to do is go there, talk to her. I ran out of my house and, without the slightest indecision, went into her building. I rang the bell. She opened the door. I started to speak, panting because I had run up the stairs. "I know you're blind, I see you all the time from my building, and I wanted to tell you that I'm your friend"–when she cut me off. "I'm not blind at all. Where did you get such an idiotic idea. Are you crazy? I don't know you from Adam." I thought I would die; I braced myself against the wall to keep from falling and closed my eyes. "What's your name?" she asked. I told her. "Go on," she continued, "tell me the whole story." There, standing in the hallway, I told her everything: "I always see you on the balcony and I've fallen in love with you." "No need to blush," she said, smiling, "and what did you do with the horn?" "It's at home." "Come," she said, "show me where you live." I followed her inside and onto the balcony, and I pointed to my apartment. We stood on the balcony; I was silent, and she laughed softly.

We went on courting at a distance, until one day she called me. "Look," she said, "we're going to run away, today, in a hurry, now, we're leaving. I know you don't have any money, but I do.

Let's go somewhere a long way from Rio, some large city where no one will find us ever again, but let's leave now, there's not a minute to waste."

In the darkness of the interstate bus I thought about everything Thirdintheworld had told me, the idiot. After I don't know how many days, I had left the house and gone to the gym. Thirdintheworld was there. He no longer worked out, he just bragged about the days when he was a contender. As soon as he saw me, he said right off: "You're skinny, yellow, kid; you need to punish that body, pump iron, pump iron. Hey, I'm getting old, they say I'm finished, but I know things. You're suffering, you've got it bad for some woman; be careful, 'cause that can destroy you like it destroyed my brother. He was a florist, and one day, when he was your age, he put a bullet in his chest in front of the house of that woman who was married and lived in Petrópolis. Hush, don't deny it, I can read it in your face, just like my brother's. You think I got to be champ just like that, for no good reason? I studied yoga, and I'm a spiritualist and a socialist (in political questions). I read other people's faces, I read other people's faces! You've got it bad, but mark what I'm telling you, no tramp is worth losing sleep over; what humiliation, a bullet in the chest. In life, a man only needs one thing: protein, protein!" While Thirdintheworld told me this, he was bugging his eyes out, clenching his teeth, punching his hands, and slapping his enormous belly. What's her name, he asked. Me: Francisca. Him: *f,* one, *r,* two, *a,* three, *n,* four, *c,* five, *i,* six, *s,* seven, *c,* eight, *a,* nine—nine letters! Run away from that woman, she's bad news for sure.

From above the window came a narrow ray of light that lit Francisca's hands, the ring, her face. The bus sped along the dark highway. She was the prettiest woman I'd ever seen in my whole life. We got to the hotel. In the room, she sat on the bed and said, "Aren't you happy?" I said I wanted to spend my entire life locked in that room with her. "We're going to stay in here as long as you want," she answered. We went to bed, totally convinced.

We stayed in that room for a week, and the only people we saw were the waiter who brought the food and the maid; we bathed together, I spoke pretty words to her, new words that I had made up, and dirty words, curse words. We rolled around in bed, and we bit each other. We rolled on the floor. One day she packed her suitcase and left without either of us saying a word.

7.

I am a man made of failure.

My search continued with Mangonga. He, at least, was happy to see me. "My friend," he said, "I have a meeting now, but we've got lots to talk about. Come by the house tonight. Nine o'clock, don't forget," and he gave me an address.

At nine o'clock I was there. Mangonga, in undershorts, opened the door to me. It was a party. "Nobody can stand this heat," he said. The others, six women and five men, also seemed to be suffering the effects of the heat, as they were all in their underwear. One woman was dancing to a macumba rhythm that was coming from the record player. My arrival was greeted with general cheer and immediately a woman grabbed my arm and said, "My name is Izete, and I'm your partner. I'm the daughter of a Japanese father and a mother from Amazonas and I have the soul of a geisha."

"Mangonga," I said, "I need to talk to you."

He stuck a glass in my hand. "We're going to talk a lot, man; not now, 'cause I'm busy, see?" and he started kissing a woman in black pants and bra and earrings so long they brushed her shoulders.

The geisha started removing my clothes. "Mangonga!" I shouted, but he had disappeared. Except for the geisha, no one paid any attention to me. People were laughing; the record player was at full volume.

Soon afterward, I'd had three glasses of the crap the geisha gave me and was shirtless and shoeless.

"What's with you?" the geisha asked.

"I need to talk with Mangonga."

"You're going to have plenty of time to talk with him. Now try to get with it. What's wrong? You don't look queer. Can't you get it up?"

I explained to her that that wasn't the case, that I needed to talk to Mangonga, that besides everything else I wasn't used to doing such things in public.

"You're not going to tell me you've never been to an orgy?"

"No. Never. All those people together, it gives me a kind of—"

"We can go off by ourselves to one of the bedrooms. This place is full of bedrooms."

"But I have to talk to Mangonga."

"You can talk later. For heaven's sake!"

"Forgive me."

"It's not forgiveness I want. Look, you can talk to Mangonga afterwards. And speaking of that, who's Mangonga?"

Before I could reply, a guy came up and said, "Enjoying yourselves?" He was dancing to the sound of the record player with a glass in his hand. "More or less," I answered. He wiggled his hips: "Tonight I'd dance to the national anthem. Want to switch women?" He pulled over a blonde who was nearby. "A blonde for a brunette. Variety, always variety, that's my philosophy of life." I turned to the geisha: "This guy wants me to trade you for the blonde." "Already? But we haven't done anything yet." "And we're not going to." "Gentleman," said the geisha to the guy dancing to the national anthem, "it's a deal."

"I need to talk to Mangonga," I told the blonde as soon as we were alone.

"Who's Mangonga? I'm never coming to another orgy. It's horrible."

"I think so too."

"Then why'd you come?"

"I need to speak with Mangonga. What about you, why did you come?"

"Who's Mangonga?"

Mangonga had vanished.

"Hello," I said to a guy in rimless glasses.

"Hello," he replied, "my hangover has kicked in ahead of time."

"Where's Mangonga?" I asked.

"What Mangonga?" he answered.

"Mangonga, the owner of the place," I explained.

"The owner isn't called Mangonga."

"What do you mean he's not called Mangonga? He invited me, opened the door for me, a guy with a big belly."

"Big belly? Almost everybody here has a big belly; even the women."

"Mangonga, the owner of the house," I insisted.

"The owner of the house is that guy over there. He's got a thing for the national anthem; he gets turned on by listening to it, can't go to bed with a woman unless he hears the national anthem. Weird guy."

"He's the owner?"

"Of course."

"What about Mangonga, the guy with the belly?"

"I've got a belly."

"His is bigger."

"I doubt it," he said, standing up. His belly was enormous; it fell onto his leg.

"You're right, yours is bigger. Where is he?"

"Who?"

"Mangonga."

"I don't know him."

I looked for him in all the rooms. No sign of Mangonga.

I went up to the guy listening to the national anthem. I shook him. "Hey, hey." He opened his eyes. "What's up, my man?"

"Do you know Mangonga?" I asked.

"What Mangonga?"

"A guy who was here at the party. He invited me."

"I don't know who he is," he said, rubbing his nose.

"Maybe you know him by another name. Are you the owner of the house?"

"Yeah."

"It was the guy who opened the door for me."

"I didn't see."

"Who were the guys you invited? Name them and I'll see if I can pick out which one is Mangonga."

"I didn't invite anyone. It was those whores who did the inviting. You better ask them."

I spoke with the five women in the living room. None of them knew Mangonga. It was as if he didn't exist.

I was half smashed. Getting smashed is a good thing. It makes you feel like closing your eyes and taking a deep breath. It was too bad the mess was so great. The owner of the house was singing the national anthem as he danced completely nude. How hot it was. That sonofabitch Mangonga had left. I went up to the guy with the geisha and said, "I want the geisha back; otherwise the party's over." "I ought to be happy," I told the geisha, as I had drunk enough for it. But I wasn't. Man is a solitary animal, an unhappy animal, and only death can fix us. Death will be my peace, Mangonga. Where did our boyhood go? It was good, it was magic, we flew, we were resurrected like Jesus Christ and we didn't have a library, or the Encyclopedia Britannica, life without complications, without religion. What an urge to cry, my dear Portuguese almond-eyed woman, let me cry on your shoulders, for the love of God, yes for the love of God, don't be shocked or push me away while I cry on your bosom, thank you, what a relief, let me sob like a child, my friend, forgetfulness, you are good, what a desire to die now, now that I'm happy, to die now that I've found—but I didn't find it, I didn't find it, what good is it to pretend, I hate people, pain is made up of small bits of relief, man is rotten. Pascal, the sewer of the universe, a chimera, it's not good pretending, tomorrow is always the same, we walk erect in the streets, bitterness devours us, and what good are small bits of relief? Damned instincts, we carefully prepare to rot, our viscera are hidden and God doesn't exist. What a (horrible) mission, what a condition.

8.

The geisha was just over five feet tall. She smiled as if she were a Balinese princess. Her eyebrows were two straight lines that rose in the direction of her temples; her hair was very fine, like that of men destined for early baldness. Her name was Izete; her favorite song was "La Vie en Rose." Her body was beige, in two tones, lighter in the belly, the buttocks, and the breasts. She wore green, by choice. She was extremely nice. She always asked, "Am I bothering you?" and I was sure that if I said yes she would disappear immediately. So I always said no; something you control can't bother you. Freckles on her nose, almond eyes; she did anything you asked, but she wasn't a robot: she was warm, had soft skin, a modulated laugh, was dexterous. She never got colds, had no venereal diseases, and didn't like politics. Her motto was to serve. She would age gracefully, loving men and the world, rich without having a penny, pretty though ugly, pure while being a whore. She would never scream at anyone or hit a child, even her own son. Money was for buying records. "And what if you don't have the money to buy records?" "What's the difference? I bought my first record when I was twenty, I'll listen to the radio." As quiet as a cat. Sometimes she wanted to talk, but she didn't even need that—"Be quiet, I want to think." It was good to think with her at my side.

9.

Everything is being recalled exactly as it happened. Roberto unapproachable. Mangonga disappeared (how to meet him again, by chance, in the street?). Felix my enemy. Only Najuba and Ulpiniano the Gentle were left. I started to fear looking for them. I was having bad luck; there's such a thing as bad luck, and the evil eye too. Sometimes it's something you have in your house, like the vase at my doctor's house. "If you tell anyone what I'm about to tell you," he said to me one day, "I'll deny it, I'll swear it's a lie and say you're crazy. This is how it was." Everything went wrong for him. His house caught on fire; his wife left him; he contracted rheumatism, which forced him to use a cane; and he fought with his colleague at the office and no new clients showed up. One day he made a house call. It was a woman who weighed seventy-five pounds, and suffered from a mysterious illness. The

worst misfortunes had happened to her: her son killed in an accident, her husband an alcoholic, the works. In her house you had
the sensation that something malevolent was about to happen at
any moment. Sinister. In the living room, on a table, was a vase
with a bird in high relief, looking at the floor. When he saw the
animal, he felt a shiver, trembled. It was just like one he had.
When he returned home, he took the vase and threw it into the
sea. "The next day, there was an undertow and several people
drowned; it was a summer Sunday." After that, his life changed:
"Just look at my house and my car outside, for you to see."

I started looking around my house for cursed objects. Could
it be a book, a painting, a knickknack? Finally I found it: a Flo-
rentine dagger, old, made to kill, kept for how many years from
exercising its function? After I got rid of it, I would be able to
look for Ulpiniano the Gentle and Najuba. I threw it in the ocean
also. There was no undertow, but several people drowned. I read
it in the paper. It was a summer Sunday. Afterward, I felt I could
go looking for Ulpiniano the Gentle and Najuba. But I didn't have
the luck I hoped for. I managed to find Ulpiniano the Gentle's
house easily enough, but he was dead.

His wife stood before me. I don't know anymore, however hard
I think about it, what she looked like—her face had no remark-
able characteristics. "When did he die?" I asked. "A month ago."
I could have caught up with him. "He's really dead, he was buried?" I couldn't accept it. "Yes. Not a single friend showed up. I
was there." "What about Vespasiano?" "Dead too." How people
just die. "And Justin?" The magician. "I couldn't find him. He
came by after the funeral." What now? "He never spoke of me?"
"Never." It wasn't possible. "That's not possible." "He never mentioned you that I can recall." It wasn't possible. "Did he speak of
the day he died and was resurrected?" "Died and was resurrected,
him, Ulpiniano?" The Gentle. "Yes, him." "Never. But he died and
was resurrected? How?" My God. "He didn't die, it was catalepsy.
You know what that is?" "No." "He never spoke of me?" "No." "Or
of Roberto, Najuba, Mangonga?" "No." My God, he never said
anything. "He didn't say anything?" "He talked, he talked, he'd

say, 'Communism saved me.' He would lie around the house, read books that left him agitated, hating people, hating the neighbor; when the neighbor bought a new car he said, 'That bastard must be exploiting someone, nobody gets rich without stealing from others, when someone makes money other wretches are losing it.' When I told him the neighbor worked like a dog, leaving the house at six in the morning and coming back at eight at night and that's why he made money, he cursed me. That's why we fought; I shouted at him that he was a bum, he didn't work, he lived off what I made, angry at people all day long, and he called me a fascist, alienated, struck me, screamed at me that communism had saved him, screamed out the window, for the neighbor to hear, that communism had saved him. Each day that went by he was different. He stopped painting, stopped creating poetry, writing, shaved once a week, wanted nothing to do with me as a woman. You don't know what I went through. But I loved him; he had wavy hair, later it turned white, but it was soft and wavy." "He can't have died, my good woman, please don't cry. I needed him, you don't know how much, now all I have left is Najuba. It's not possible that he never spoke of our time in high school, go on, answer!'"

10.

I couldn't have had a greater surprise. That was why finding Najuba had been so difficult. He had changed his name and become a recluse. He'd shaved his head.

I climbed the hill to get to where he lived. I was worn out when I arrived; I wasn't what I used to be, I was short of breath, could feel my heart beating. He received me without surprise. He seemed to be the same boy from 20 years ago. (He was maybe thinner.)

He didn't gesticulate as he talked, as in the past; he kept his hands together. His voice was deep; he gave the impression of an artist with a very well applied talent.

"I can feel that you need me," he said. I said I did, that I needed him. "I've got it in my head that youth is an illusion. Did you ever hear anything more screwed up?" Brother Euzébio (this was what Najuba called himself now) answered, "The only reality is our imagination."

"Berkeley. He was a bishop."

"Anglican."

"Does God exist, or is he in our imagination?"

"Men without imagination cannot reach God. God exists."

"I don't know. Now, here in this silence, in this old monastery, I don't know. But on other occasions I *know* he doesn't exist."

We sat in a courtyard, under a tree. The wind lightly stirred the leaves.

"I need to find out whether the things of our youth actually existed or are the product of my imagination. Neither Roberto, Mangonga, Felix, nor Ulpiniano the Gentle could help me. You're the only one left, Najuba, sorry, Euzébio. Brother Euzébio. I need to know, it's driving me mad."

Then I asked Najuba, Brother Euzébio, if he remembered the death of Ulpiniano the Gentle, Roberto's flying, Mangonga's links to diabolical things. He remembered everything.

"I remember, I remember," he said softly.

"You know I spoke with Roberto, and he didn't seem to remember anything."

"No one likes to recall the sins of childhood."

"Sins."

"He stole the airplane, didn't he?"

"What airplane?"

"The single-engine plane that he stole from the aviation club, to prove he was capable of flying an aircraft without ever having taken a lesson."

"But I wasn't referring to that. I didn't even know he stole a plane. I mean the day he flew, when his body left the ground, eight inches or more. You don't remember that? Levitation, he was doing experiments in levitation, and he suspended his own body in space."

Najuba, Brother Euzébio, looked at me in embarrassment. No, he didn't remember that. And what about the death of Ulpiniano the Gentle? He remembered, but it had all been a joke, hadn't it? No one can come back from the dead. But it was a case of catalepsy, like any other miracle, I replied. Najuba remained silent. He didn't remember anything, that was the truth, he didn't remember anything; he didn't want to, or couldn't, remember anything. He had broken with the past, the lead weight on his penis, the cruelties of youth; he wanted to leave all that behind and build his new life as a saint. What good did it do for me to ask if he remembered a thing he wanted to forget? The one who wanted to remember, who didn't want to build anything new, was me.

11.

Thought is the fastest thing there is. I have the impression that I no longer have any mission to accomplish. I feel, now, enormous lethargy, and I let myself listen to the sounds of the night. Some of them come from the street, but I attach no importance to those. The really serious sounds come from inside the house. The majority of them are not identifiable. Ghosts? I just heard a creak, but that doesn't make me nervous: I hand myself over to the roaches. Thieves? I'm so tired that I no longer want to know about anything. Let them steal everything. Let them kill me; they don't frighten me anymore. A door slammed. I listen with the ears of the tubercular: I hear the tick-tock of my wristwatch on the night table. Did I lock the doors? I don't want to think about it. I have spent my life thinking about locking the doors. In any case, despite the enormous doubt, I know that I locked them. And the windows too, the shutters, everything. Everything locked. But I hear a different noise. Perhaps the lightest of feet carrying a frail body, and another heart beating, and another lung breathing. I won't think about the past anymore. I know.

ACCOUNT OF THE INCIDENT

EARLY ON THE MORNING on May 3 a brown cow was crossing the bridge over the Coroado River, at marker 53, in the direction of Rio de Janeiro.

A passenger bus of the Única Auto Ônibus firm, license plates RF-80-07-83 and JR-81-12-27, was crossing the Coroado bridge in the direction of São Paulo.

When he saw the cow, the driver, Plínio Sérgio, tried to avoid hitting it. He collided with the cow, and then the bus hit the side of the bridge and plunged into the river.

On the bridge, the cow was dead.

Under the bridge, the dead were: a woman dressed in a long skirt and a yellow blouse, she appeared to be about twenty, who would never be identified; Ovídia Monteiro, thirty-four years old; Manuel dos Santos Pinhal, a thirty-five-year-old Portuguese whose papers identified him as a member of the Beverage Manufacturing Employees Union; the child Reinaldo, age one year, Manuel's son; and Eduardo Varela, married, forty-three years old.

The accident was witnessed by Elias Gentil dos Santos and his wife Lucília, residents in the vicinity. Elias tells his wife to fetch a large knife from home. "A knife?" Lucília asks. "A knife, quick, you idiot," says Elias. He is worried. Ah! Lucília understands. Lucília leaves, running.

Marcílio da Conceição appears. Elias looks at him with hatred. Ivonildo de Moura Júnior also appears. And that fool hasn't brought a knife! thinks Elias. He is angry at everyone; his hands tremble. Elias spits on the ground several times, strongly, until his mouth is dry.

"Hello, Mr. Elias," says Marcílio. "Hello," says Elias between clenched teeth, looking to the sides. That mulatto! thinks Elias.

"It's really something," says Ivonildo, leaning on the bridge railing and looking at the firefighters and police below. Only Elias, Marcílio, Ivonildo, and the driver of a car from the Highway Patrol are on the bridge.

"Situation ain't goin' too good," says Elias, looking at the cow. He can't take his eyes off the cow.

"That's true," says Marcílio.

The three men look at the cow.

In the distance they see Lucília, running toward them.

Elias spits again. "If I could, I'd be rich too," says Elias. Marcílio and Ivonildo nod their heads and look at the cow, and at Lucília, who approaches in a run. Lucília is also unhappy to see the two men. "Good morning, Dona Lucília," says Marcílio. Lucília responds with a nod of her head. "Did I take a long time?" she asks her husband, panting.

Elias takes the knife in his hand, as if it were a dagger; he looks with hatred at Marcílio and Ivonildo. He spits on the ground. He leaps onto the cow.

"The filet's in the rear," says Lucília. Elias begins cutting up the cow.

Marcílio approaches. "Will you lend me your knife afterwards, Mr. Elias?" "No," Elias replies.

Marcílio withdraws, moving quickly. Ivonildo runs away at top speed.

"They're going to get knives," says Elias angrily, "that mulatto, that sonofabitch." His hands, his shirt, and his pants are soaked in blood. "You should've brought a bag, a sack, two sacks, you imbecile. Go get a couple of sacks," Elias orders.

Lucília dashes away.

Elias has already cut two large chunks of meat when, running, Marcílio and his wife Dalva, Ivonildo and his mother-in-law Aurélia, and Erandir Medrado and his brother Valfrido Medrado appear. All are carrying knives and machetes. They attack the cow.

Lucília reappears, running. She can hardly speak. She is eight months pregnant, suffers from worms, and her house is on top of a hill and the bridge at the top of another hill. Lucília has brought a second knife with her. Lucília cuts into the cow.

"Somebody lend me a knife or I'll arrest all of you," says the driver of the patrol car. The Medrado brothers, who have brought several knives, lend one to the driver.

Carrying a saw, a machete, and a small axe, João Leitão, the butcher, appears, accompanied by two helpers.

"You can't," shouts Elias.

João Leitão kneels down near the cow.

"You can't," says Elias, shoving João. João falls down.

"You can't," the Medrado brothers shout.

"You can't," shouts everyone except the police driver.

João moves away; he stops ten yards off and watches with his helpers.

Half the cow's flesh has been removed. It wasn't easy to cut off the tail. No one succeeded in cutting off the head or the hooves. And no one wanted the guts.

Elias has filled two sacks. The other men use their shirts as sacks.

Elias and his wife are the first to leave. "Cook me up a thick steak," he tells Lucília, smiling. "I'm going to ask Dona Dalva for some potatoes, I'm going to make you French fries too," replies Lucília.

The remains of the cow lie in a pool of blood. João whistles to one of his two helpers. One of them brings a wheelbarrow. The remains of the cow are placed in the wheelbarrow. Nothing is left on the bridge but the pool of blood.

PRIDE

ON VARIOUS OCCASIONS he had heard it said that the major events of a drowning person's life pass through his mind with vertiginous rapidity, and he'd always found that statement absurd, until one day it happened that he was dying, and as he died he remembered forgotten things, from the newspaper article that said he'd worn shoes with holes in them, without socks, and painted his big toe to hide the hole, during his impoverished childhood, but he had always worn socks and shoes without holes in them, socks that his mother carefully darned, and he remembered the very smooth wooden darning egg that she would insert into the socks and darn, darning all the years of his childhood, and he remembered how since he was a child he didn't like to drink water and if he drank a whole glass he couldn't catch his breath, and so he would go the entire day without drinking a drop of liquid because he didn't have the money for juices and soda, and that sometimes his mother would make a drink out of Kolynos toothpaste, but there wasn't always toothpaste in the house, and at the moment he was dying he also remembered all the women he loved, or almost all of them, and also the red wooden parquet floor in a house where he had lived, but he was anguished because he couldn't recall what house that was, and also the cheap pocket watch that broke the first day he used it, and also the blue flannel jacket, and the pain that made him crawl along the floor, and the doctor saying he needed to do an X-ray of his urinary ducts, and the closer death came the more the old memories mixed with the recent ones, him arriving late at the doctor's office, who was already dressed to leave, he'd already sent his nurse home, and the doctor in a hurry, as anxious as someone who's on his way to meet a very desirable sweetheart, telling him to take off his coat, roll up his sleeves, and lie down on a metal table, explaining that after all the X-ray wouldn't take long, it was just a matter of injecting the contrast and taking the pictures, and the doctor leaned over the table to apply the contrast in the vein of his arm and he smelled the delicate scent of his cologne and noticed his polka-dot tie, and it wasn't long before he felt his larynx contracting and cutting off his breathing and he tried to tell the doctor but he couldn't utter a sound and all the memories came into his mind, the newspaper article, the blue jacket, the wood floor, the women, his mother's smooth darning egg, while in one corner of the office the doctor was talking on the phone in a low voice, and because he knew he was dying he pounded forcefully on the metal table, the doctor was alarmed and began nervously rummaging through the cabinet drawers, cursing, blaming the nurse and telling him to stay calm, that he was going to give him an antiallergic injection but he couldn't find the damned medicine, and he thought I'm suffocating to death, life and death running side by side, and, conscious that his death was imminent and inevitable, he remembered the words of a poem, I will die but that is all I will do for death, for he had always refused to let it clutch at his heart, and in that moment when he was dying he would not let it take over his soul, for the most that Death would have of him was the dead man, and so he thought about life, about the women he had known, his mother darning his socks, the smooth darning egg, the newspaper article, and he pounded on the table, bang! bang! bang!, I'm thinking about my mother, and at that moment the doctor, not knowing what to do, in torment, and startled by the noisy blows he was striking on the metal table, looked at him with great sympathy and sadness, and he screamed again bang! bang! that he forgave the doctor, bang! bang!, that he forgave everyone, when his mind ran swiftly through the remembrances of life, and the doctor, now overcome by his helplessness, desperate and confused, removed his shoes, and he raised his head and noticed the black socks on his feet, and saw in the sock on his right foot a hole through which appeared a piece of his big toe, and he remembered how his mother was proud and that he himself was also very proud and that had always been his ruination and his salvation, and he thought, I'm not going to die here with a hole in my sock, that's not going to be the final picture that I leave for the world, and he contracted every muscle in his body, twisted on the table like a scorpion burning in the flames and by brute force succeeded in making air penetrate his larynx with a terrifying sound, and the air being expelled from his lungs made an even more brutish and frightening sound, and he escaped Death and thought about nothing else. The doctor, seated in a chair, wiped the sweat from his face. He got up from the metal table and put on his shoes.

THE NOTEBOOK

AFTER MY SEPARATION I bought a little notebook where I would write the names of the women who went to bed with me.

When I was married I didn't have a notebook; my wife was very possessive, and her attacks of jealousy, in addition to lasting a long time, were quite theatrical. She would tear up my new clothes. I couldn't have cared less.

I hid the existence of the other women who populated my world from Nice. I still didn't have a notebook in those days, but I did go to bed with other women. Nice's jealousy was always caused by some innocent gesture on my part, such as looking at a woman who was passing by our table in a restaurant. Sometimes, as a mere speculative exercise, I would imagine what she'd do if she knew I screwed other women. But I didn't take chances. Address books, letters, photos, clandestine things like that are always discovered.

Why did I leave her? Maybe because I couldn't take having to wear the clothes—"the latest style"—that Nice would buy for me. I had been laughing at myself in those clothes for some time. I have a sense of humor, like every lazy guy. I remember a dinner, with the usual types who get dolled up for such occasions present, when one of the women, a good-looking redhead, complimented me on my outfit. I said that Nice had chosen it. The redhead turned to her husband, a formally dressed lawyer who, despite the air conditioning, was sweating like crazy and told him he should follow my example. The rest of the night, the couples—among them professionals, businessmen, even an artist, the majority dressed according to the fashion dictates of the time—discussed whether wives should or shouldn't choose the clothes their husbands wore. It was a heated and extended debate; the talkative lawyer, who didn't like me, was one of the most eloquent.

The next day I packed my old clothes and some books, the poetry ones, and moved out. My ex-wife was so ingenuous that she ripped all the new clothes that I'd left in the apartment to pieces, thinking that she'd gotten her revenge, and then she hired the idiot lawyer who sweated at the dinner to bleed me, but he got less than she wanted. My union with Nice had lasted three years, fed by inertia, that passive quality that makes a guy resist, whatever the reading on the Richter scale, the routine seismic jolts of every marriage.

I'm slothful. But my laziness never got in the way of my drive to seduce and possess women. I just don't want to get married again. In life, motivation is everything. It's a psychic energy, as the researchers say, a tension that sets the human organism in motion and determines our behavior. Sometimes I think that, in my case, it's also a curse.

What women did I want to seduce? Famous ones? They didn't interest me. A famous woman, whatever her type of celebrity, usually has more flaws than appeal, no matter how pretty she might be. Rich women? Zero motivation. Cultured? Zero motivation. Elegant? That's interesting, but not enough—obviously, I'm not talking about clothes; elegance is something else. The outdoorsy type? What for, to run along the beach with me with one of those heart monitors taped to my chest? Zero, obviously. I wanted pretty, cheerful women. That's all. Of course, if she was just a little bit on the plain side but had a great body she went into the notebook. In fact, a good body was more important than a pretty face.

What difficulties did I encounter in acquiring the stable listed in my notebook? I wanted pretty women, but sometimes it happened that the pretty woman was also intelligent. Theoretically, an intelligent woman would see right away that I'm a womanizer. But in practice they're even bigger fools than the stupid ones. Like, for example, the latest one, called Safira, to go into my notebook.

Before going on, I have to say that I like to screw a woman the day after I meet her—haste is the enemy of perfection. This is in fact one of my favorite clichés; I'm not uncomfortable using commonplace expressions, they're always the clearest conception of a reality, even if they're worn out by overuse. But, as I was saying, at the second encounter with Safira, as was my custom, I suggested we go to bed.

"Don't you think we ought to wait for the right time?"

I always have a good cliché up my sleeve.

"Boire sans soif et faire l'amour en tout temps, madame, il n'y a que ça qui nous distingue des autres bêtes. Beaumarchais, *Mariage de Figaro,"* I replied.

I forgot to mention that I speak French; any slouch can learn French. Safira was young and didn't know that ancient bromide or the author of the play, just Mozart's opera. She knew very little French, but as she was reasonably intelligent she understood that I'd spoken the truth: what distinguishes us from the animals is that we drink when we're not thirsty and make love at any time. It's part of human nature, of our essence. So, Safira understood that she should follow her purest instincts and went to bed with me. I could put her name in the notebook, along with a short comment about her major characteristics.

I could relate countless other affairs, but I'm afraid I'm becoming prolix. But I can't pass up the opportunity to speak of Andressa—a difficult case.

Andressa was the daughter of nouveau riche parents—in that social circle no one gives their daughter a name like Maria. She avoided going to bed with me the first day, the second, the third, and even—incredible, isn't it?—the fourth.

"Is that how you see women? How you see me? As a sex object?" she asked after my latest attempt.

I protested vehemently, said I was attracted by her physical, mental, and moral attributes, by her overall personality.

I saw that my categorical affirmative hadn't convinced her. She still had strong doubts about me, whether I deserved her trust or not.

For a lazy man like me, that difficulty can be a disincentive. But, as I said, my motivation, or curse, was as strong as that of Sisyphus.

With great effort I persuaded her to meet with me again, in my apartment. On the critical day, I forgot the notebook with the names of the women, on whose red cover was written *The Women I Have Loved,* on the living room coffee table.

And what couldn't help but happen, happened. Andressa found the notebook and picked it up—it couldn't be missed, with its garish cover. Women are curious, as we know, and such clandestine things are always discovered by them. Woe to him who doesn't know this.

"The women I've loved," said Andressa, reading the cover of the notebook.

I was nearby. I ran over and snatched the red notebook from her hands.

"Sorry," I said nervously, "but this book contains things that I wouldn't like you to read. Sorry."

"Why? What's in it, besides names?"

"Well . . ."

"What else?"

I put the book in my pocket and brought my hands together, as if in prayer, in the best style of an Italian supplicant: "Please, don't ask me to let you read this notebook."

"Women's names . . ." Andressa repeated, disdainfully. "And what else does that thing contain, that I can't read?"

I ran my hands over my head and remained calm. I was unable to hide my embarrassment; I think I even blushed.

"Go on, say it. What's in there, besides names?"

"The . . . uh . . . characteristics . . . of each of them."

"How sordid. You write down the obscenities you do with the women you claim to have loved in your notebook?"

"It's not like that."

Andressa got her purse, which she had left on a chair.

"I never knew anyone could be such a lowlife."

When she was at the door, about to leave, I took the notebook out of my pocket.

"You can read it. Please, don't leave."

She stopped, undecided.

"I don't want to read that trash."

"Now you have to read it. After all those horrible things you said about me, I at least deserve for you to honor this request. Give me a chance to prove that I'm a man of character. I love you."

I rubbed my eyes, like someone on the verge of tears.

"Like you loved the dozens of women in your little book?"

"Read it, I'm begging you."

I handed the book to Andressa.

She hesitated for a moment. She started to read, and little by little her face began to soften. She moved to the middle of the living room and put her purse back on the chair.

"There are only five names," said Andressa.

"Read what's written there," I said.

"I've read it. Forgive me," said Andressa.

"I'll only forgive you if you read it aloud,"

Andressa read:

"'Marta: Likes cats and watches sunsets. Sílvia: Concerned with ecology. Luíza: Loves the lyricism of Florbela Espanca. Renata: Sings Cole Porter songs better than anyone. Lourdes: Has a beautiful orchid collection.' There are only these five?"

"Six, now, with you, who'll close out that book for good."

"Who is Florbela?"

"A Portuguese poet."

"Will you forgive me?"

"Of course. The blame for the misunderstanding was entirely mine."

"My name isn't in the book yet. What are you going to write?"

I took the book from her hand and wrote, "Andressa: Sophisticated, generous, intelligent, as beautiful as a fairy tale princess."

Andressa read what I had written for her. She hugged me affectionately. We went to bed.

She spent the night with me. As we were having sex she called me "my love" several times.

In the morning, when she left, I got the notebook, which Andressa had left on the coffee table, and put it in a locked drawer with the other notebook, the real one, which had a discreet gray cover and contained a summary of the real peculiarities and the names of the dozens of women I'd had. The one with the red cover, which Andressa had read, was a forgery that I had prepared specifically for that arduous undertaking. Five whole days!

In my best calligraphy, I wrote in the gray notebook: "Andressa: Goes down. Anal. Cellulite. Never heard of Florbela Espanca."

THE ELEVENTH OF MAY

Breakfast, lunch, and the afternoon snack are served in the cubicles. It's an enormous job, carrying lunch pails and mugs to each cubicle. There must be a reason for that.

The cubicle has a bed, a closet, a chamber pot, and a television set. The TV is on all day. There must be a reason for that also. The programs are transmitted by closed circuit from somewhere in the Home. Old soap operas, broadcast unceasingly.

Today a Brother took away the radio that Baldomero was putting together. His daughter had brought him the parts. Listening is permitted, the Brother said, but leisure must not be a source of injustice, here everyone must have the same things. There went Baldomero's little toy.

Baldomero, before he retired, was an electrical engineer. He claims to have invented a technique for distributing electricity underground called a polymuriform system. I am, I mean I was, a history professor, and my technological knowledge is minimal, so I don't know if he's telling the truth—old people lie a lot. Baldomero's retirement left him very depressed. Before coming here he was put in a leisure adaptation clinic where, he says without malice, they treated him with electric shocks. Given his profession, they must not have been the first ones he received. We came to the Eleventh of May around the same time. He is a depressed man; someday he'll kill himself. It's common for old people to kill themselves, because of the melancholy of idleness, loneliness, disease. Ninety percent of people over sixty suffer from some disease.

———

I'm sitting in the courtyard with Baldomero and a guy named Pharoux, who was a policeman. Pharoux is missing an eye, which he lost in a street fight, according to what he says. He's a man of few words, suspicious, thin, his face furrowed with deep lines. The missing eye is covered with a black patch. He looks like a TV pirate; I feel like telling him that, but I know he has no sense of humor so I keep quiet.

From where I am I can see the smokestack of the garbage furnace spewing smoke into the air. The smoke is black. I wonder what kind of garbage they burn. Remains of food, soiled paper? The smoke turns white.

"They've just chosen a new Pope," I say.

Pharoux looks at me gravely. I laugh, but he remains serious. A man with a strong personality and bad character.

———

On one of the courtyard walls is written: Life is Beautiful. Also written there is: The Time Has Come to Reap.

"Do you know what it is we're going to reap?" I ask Baldomero.

"Pre-chewed marmalade," Baldomero says.

"Yawns," I say. I was going to say: death; that's the reaping that awaits us. But a torpid, lazy, bored old man can only open his mouth to yawn.

I yawn, opening my mouth as wide as I can. I ask Baldomero if he knows how many of us there are in the Eleventh of May Home.

He doesn't know.

No one knows. Maybe the fat director knows.

There are sixty cubicles on my floor.

"Hello, Guilherme," I say, sticking my head in the first one.

Guilherme grins at me, displaying his gray gums. He's lying in bed watching television.

I have a list with the names of all the occupants of the cubicles in my wing. There are sixty cubicles. No one knows I have the list.

I enter them one by one.

"Hello, Moura."

But it's not Moura who's there, sitting on the chamber pot, watching television. It's another old man. He says his name is Aristides. I write down Aristides's date of admission. It's the date Moura left.

Moura lasted a month. But before he disappeared and made way for another inmate, Moura began shuffling aimlessly through the corridors. He no longer heard what was said to him, didn't shave, and finally wouldn't get out of bed, claiming weakness and pains in his legs.

"What were you talking about?" asks the Brother.

Pharoux and I are sitting on the same bench in the courtyard. I don't know why, but when I saw Pharoux I sat down beside him.

"We're not talking," Pharoux says.

"Why aren't you watching television?" the Brother asks politely. "Recreation time in the courtyard is over."

The Brothers never become impatient.

"I don't like television," Pharoux says.

"Come, come," says the Brother pleasantly, taking my arm and leading me to the cubicle, "it's time to rest."

I'm lying in the cubicle. There's no way to turn the damned television off. The sets are controlled remotely, from the same place from which the image is broadcast.

The Brother brought me to the room as if I were a little old man. As if I were a little old man, I allowed him to. He didn't want me to talk further with Pharoux. He didn't mess with Pharoux. Is he afraid of Pharoux? To be sure, if the Brother didn't want us talking and if I had already been led away, it was better for him to leave Pharoux in peace, as he did.

Pharoux said we weren't talking, but it wasn't true. We were talking.

"I only sleep at night," Pharoux had said.

"I sleep in the daytime and at night. All I have to do is lie down and I go to sleep right away," I replied.

"That's what they want. The more you sleep, the more you want to sleep. One day you don't wake up."

Pharoux had just said that when the Brother came up.

The Director calls me to see him. His office is in a tower—it's the same height as the garbage furnace smokestack, but it's on the other side. The Home is a two-story building divided into eight wings of sixty cubicles each. This is a deduction; I only have access to one of the wings, my own, on the second floor. There are four wings on the first floor and four on the second, possibly each with sixty cubicles like mine. I think so. A square. In the middle is the courtyard, on one side the smokestack and on the other the director's tower. An ugly and sad-looking building.

The Director is a young, fat man. With the exception of the inmates, everyone is young at the Eleventh of May.

"How are you doing?" the Director asks.

He uses the polite form of address with me to feign a respect that he doesn't really feel. They are all very well trained.

"I'm all right."

"Is there something you wish to mention, some complaint?"

"No, no complaint."

The Director stands up, first taking a piece of paper from the desk. I don't know how he fits into his chair, which has two projections on each side to support his elbows. His ass is very big. I remain alert, hoping he'll turn his back so I can see his large, flabby bottom. My bottom is skinny and loose, like an old cat's.

"I have some information here . . ."

He pretends to read the paper.

"You haven't been following the Rules of the Home. Now look, the Rules are made to protect the residents, drawn up by doctors and psychologists for the good of all, understand? Nevertheless, I see here that you wander through the corridors during the evening rest period, visiting other residents in their rooms . . . That isn't good for you or for anyone, understand? It's against the Rules."

"Now that I think of it, I do have a complaint," I say.

"A complaint? Well, well, please state it."

"The food. It's not good and it doesn't seem very nutritious."

"It's the same food that's eaten in the barracks, in the factories, in the schools, in the cooperatives, in the ministries, everywhere. The country is going through a difficult time. Do you think that the retired should eat better than those who are producing? Of course you don't. Besides, the food served at the Eleventh of May follows the criteria laid down by the dietitian, bearing in mind the residents' particular bodily needs."

The Director turns around and goes to his chair. I don't see how he manages to squeeze himself into the chair. It must be hard for him to get into his clothes too.

"Watery soup," I say.

"Not everyone has a lot of teeth like you . . . Soft food is easier to swallow . . . We have to place the welfare of the majority above all else. The majority, you understand, the majority."

He spoke for some ten minutes about the needs of the majority: rest and mush. He ended with a warning. He doesn't have to show his true face; I know something about history, I know when I'm being threatened. That wasn't what he said, it was I who said it, or rather thought it. To tell the truth, the phrase isn't mine, I'm quoting, but I don't remember the source. Ecmnesia. The Director said:

"I don't want you going into the others' rooms, all right? Otherwise, unfortunately and against my wishes, I will be obliged to discontinue your breakfast. It's the Rules."

———

I have a lot of teeth, but they're false, almost all of them, and they balance precariously in my mouth. But better false teeth than none at all. I recognize that.

Another thing I discussed with Pharoux:

"What do you like to do best? The thing that interests you the most, if you still have interests," I asked. I laughed but he didn't.

"Eating," Pharoux said.

"But the food here is no good," I said.

"It's no good," Pharoux said, "but I eat all they give me, to stay alive. If you don't eat, you die."

———

There is no doctor in the Home to take care of the inmates when they get sick. One or another of the Brothers tends to us, always by giving us a painkiller, whatever our illness. I often have intestinal problems, strong attacks of diarrhea that come on unexpectedly. When I went to complain, the Brother gave me an aspirin.

"You're not well yet but you're going to be. Till then use the night vessel."

I could have died sitting on the chamber pot, if Cortines hadn't found some medicine for me. Cortines is full of tricks. He was a physical education teacher. Whenever I go into his cubicle he's working out. I don't know where he gets the medicine and the extra food. He's funny.

"A young man doesn't need to work out," he said one day when I found him doing sit-ups in his cubicle.

But an old man does. The older he is, the more working out. It's not to live longer, it's to stay on his feet while he's still alive.

"My misfortune," he continued, "was being unable to deal with the upper levels of the sports authority. So they put me here to burn out slowly, like a candlewick. But I'll be burning for a long time."

Cortines laughs. It must be his muscles that make him laugh so loud.

Cortines is entirely bald. Every day he carefully shaves the few hairs he has. His arms and neck are hard, bony, sharp.

———

Tonight I dreamed I was Malesherbes. I walked peacefully to the guillotine, after having carefully wound my watch. They wanted to kill me because I insisted on calling Louis XVI "His Majesty." But I called him that not because I liked or respected him, but because, being old, I believed I had the right to oppose the power holders, who were sitting on top of the world. Or rather atop the guillotine. In the dream.

Why do I dream of Malesherbes and not of Getúlio Vargas, or of Pedro I, or of Tiradentes?

Pharoux carries around a steel knife. What the devil does he want with a weapon like that? Pharoux always has a hostile air to him; his face seems to say: hatred is the greatest and most lasting of pleasures. Someone once said that human beings love quickly but hate slowly. I wonder who it is that Pharoux hates. It must have been pretty bad to fall into his hands in his policeman days.

The history of France is more interesting than the history of Brazil, is that it?

———

Experience (or history itself) teaches that people and governments never learn anything from history. The same way, we old people never learn anything from our experience. That's an idiotic phrase: if youth knew, if age could. Why is it that we old ones can't? Because they won't let us, that's the only reason.

I tell this to Baldomero. But he's not listening. His depression has grown deeper and deeper. Cortines and Pharoux are more attentive, but they're very ignorant. Talking with them has little appeal; they don't understand what I say. One day Pharoux asked me what history was and I replied, joking and quoting I don't remember who (ecmnesia, my memory isn't what it used to be), that history is something that never happened, written by someone who wasn't there. He said he didn't understand. If it didn't happen, how is it history? he asked. Pharoux lacks imagination that way. But when I said that the Director had called me in he became very interested.

"What did you tell him?"

"Nothing. I didn't mention your knife."

"If you do, you die, you old fool," he said.

———

The inmate who's been longest in the Home, in my wing, is Cortines. Six months. All the others who had been here longer have disappeared. Did they die? Were they transferred? Nobody worries about inmate turnover; after all, no one makes friends here in this place. Only I secretly follow, in the four months I've been here, the coming and going of the inmates. A professional failing.

I asked one of the Brothers, I don't remember his name—they're all alike and never stay on the same wing for long—what was done with the bodies of those who died. He was very surprised by the question. And suspicious.

"What? What do you mean by that?"

"Many here have no family, or if they have family, their relatives aren't interested in them, almost nobody has visitors. In our wing only Baldomero was visited by his daughter, and even then only once. When they die I have the impression that the lack of interest continues, and as I said, many have no relatives and therefore . . ."

"And therefore what?"

"I mean, I'm thinking of my own case. I have no one, if I die who's going to bury me?"

The Brother seemed relieved.

"The Institute, of course. The Institute pays the expenses, don't worry about those things. Come along, come along, watch some television, enjoy yourself, don't worry yourself needlessly."

He went into my room with me and stood watching the soap opera for ten minutes.

Before leaving he eyed me from the entrance to the cubicle. I pretended to pay attention to the television until he left.

———

The cubicles have no doors. Old people are deaf and the television sets play at very high volume. Since there's just one program, the sound surrounds you, springing from every corner, but that doesn't prevent the inmates from going to sleep the moment they enter their cubicles and watch the screen for a few minutes.

I'm carrying the papers with the names and dates of admission and departure of the inmates in my wing beneath my undershirt. I don't know why I do this. From time to time they clean the cubicles and make the inmate leave. Two Brothers always come. They look through all the papers, seize all the books; it's not a cleaning at all, it's a search, a kind of spying.

The inmates always die at night. Lins had a fractured leg (our balance is shaky and our bones are weak), and would drag himself out of the bed, which is low, to the chamber pot, or else he would defecate and urinate right in the bed. I passed by the door of his cubicle one afternoon and a nauseating smell of shit and gangrene was coming from inside. Lins was lying in bed watching television. The next morning the cubicle was empty and smelled of disinfectant.

When I see someone coughing and moaning, or else very quiet in his bed, I know that in the morning his cubicle will be empty. I'm not saying they were killed or anything of that nature; the Institute wouldn't do something like that. I'm old and know that every old person is mildly paranoid, and I don't want to invent persecutions and nonexistent crimes. Who said that history is a lying account of crimes and tragedies? I'm beginning to lose myself, it must be arteriosclerosis; I start to think about something and my thoughts wander. And how bad my memory is! Ecmnesia. Ah yes, the papers underneath my shirt. No, that's not it. It's the fact of old people being sent here to die. Perhaps old people on their last legs, with a short life expectancy, are brought here. That would explain why they all die in such a short time. Or could it be something else, a broader plan, a policy for all of us?

In short, I don't have much time.

That thought numbs my body, as if I had already ceased to exist. I feel neither pain nor sadness, merely a kind of dread—the dread of one who no longer has a body and lacks the solid notion of inhabiting a form, a structure, a volume. As if I had lost the material and become spirit alone, or mind. That's impossible. But it's what I felt when, without pain or other agonies forewarning my end, I suspected for the first time that I might have only a few months to live.

———

I now make my rounds cautiously. The Brothers, in spite of being young, are lazy, and after lunch they like to rest—even those on duty do so. They also have a television in their room, and they watch other programs that are not broadcast to us. I know, through questions I ask innocently, that they fall asleep in front of the set too. Television is very interesting, leaving out sleep and forgetfulness. I can't remember the things I see.

Baldomero isn't well. When I enter his cubicle he greets me with incomprehensible words. "Magnete magneticusque corporibus . . . Aepinus, Faraday, Volta, Ampère . . ."

"Are you all right, Baldomero?" I ask.

"Ohmmm . . . Ohmmm," he responds, droning with his mouth shut as if he were a worn out buzzer. I can't resist and burst out laughing. The more I laugh, the more he buzzes. How cruel human beings are! Baldomero has gone mad and here I am laughing at his insanity. Then he points to the television set and yells, "Jenkins, Jenkins!"

"Jenkins!" His screams finally attract the attention of the Brothers. They try to take him to the infirmary, but he resists. His body seems galvanized (no pun intended, as I no longer find humor in what is happening) by an unexpected force. It takes three Brothers to subdue him. He is finally carried off to the infirmary.

I know I will be punished for having been found in Baldomero's cubicle. But that doesn't bother me. What depresses me is having mocked Baldomero. I weep with repentance. I know that my copious weeping is one more symptom of my old age; I'm unhappy, afraid, and feel an unbearable urge to eat a piece of chocolate candy, which makes my mouth water. Without ceasing to cry, I drool from the corners of my lips. I look at my whimpering, spittle-covered face in the cubicle mirror: a figure at once ridiculous and repulsive. Is it really me? Was it for this that I lived so many years?

The afternoon snack is just a cup of coffee with a piece of bread. It's served at five o'clock. If for any reason I delay falling asleep (which is rare), the hunger becomes intolerable and I dream about breakfast, which is served at six. Black coffee with bread.

The brother with the coffee cart passes by my door in the morning without stopping. I feel like running after him and asking for a piece of bread. But I restrain myself. Enough of crumbs, of degradation. I am feeling anger; one who feels anger doesn't need to drink coffee, doesn't need bread.

The Director calls me to his office. On the outside he is the same patient person as always, it's his mask. But I know that he detests me; it's a subtle perception which penetrates his pretense. "Baldomero passed away. A heart attack," the Director says.

"I am obliged to tell you that we think you contributed to the fatal attack," the Director says.

"Contributed how?"

"Baldomero was an excitable person. Your going to his room, at an inappropriate hour, must have been bad for him, his health was very precarious. I am obliged to tell you that your irregular behavior worries us."

"Baldomero was dying of hunger and unhappiness, like all of us here," I say.

"Hunger? For your information, the nation spends a substantial part of its resources on inactive elderly people. If we tried to keep all the retirees well-fed and happy, through costly preventive medicine programs, occupational therapy, recreation, and leisure, the nation's total resources would be consumed by the task. Don't you know the country is going through one of the gravest economic crises in its entire history? We were once a nation of youth and little by little we're becoming a nation of the old."

"Young people get older," I say. "You'll be old someday."

The Director looks at me for some time. His interest in me appears to have ended, as if I were a hopeless case.

"Behave yourself," he says affably, but without interest, and dismisses me with a vague gesture.

"Was Baldomero's daughter advised?" I ask as I leave.

"Daughter? Oh yes," says the Director, absentmindedly.

For lunch I had a vile soup. Even so, I have diarrhea. I ask a Brother for medicine. He takes a long time, but he finally brings a capsule and leaves, after making sure I swallowed it.

"You'll be okay now," he says.

The capsule he brought me is different from the pills I usually take. That's why I pretended to take it, leaving it hidden in my hand.

———

I show the capsule to Pharoux. I ask if he's seen one like it before among the medication they give us.

He doesn't reply. He says he wants to be alone. We old people have a tendency toward misanthropy. Besides, Pharoux is suspicious, wary of me.

I look up Cortines. As always, he's working out. Cortines carefully opens the capsule. Inside is a white powder. Cortines puts a very tiny amount on the tip of his tongue.

"To me this is poison," Cortines says.

"How do you know?"

Cortines doesn't know. He suspects.

Cortines has bread and cheese on his bed. The two of us eat. He refuses to tell me where he gets the supplies. He must steal them. Cortines stays near the door while we eat, on the lookout for Brothers.

"Careful, here comes one of them."

———

BROTHER: What are you doing here?

ME: Watching television.

BROTHER (*Very affably*): Ah, very good, that's the way. Television is a very good thing, it amuses, educates; if I could, I'd watch television all day, like you. What's your name again?

ME: José.

BROTHER: Look, José, you should watch television in your own quarters. Have you been here long?

ME: No.

BROTHER: But I looked for you a half hour ago and didn't find you.

ME: I was in the courtyard looking at the trees.

BROTHER: Fine, fine, trees are made to be looked at and admired. We have over ten trees in our courtyard, we're proud of the fact.

All this time I was holding the remains of the capsule in my hand.

BROTHER: How are your intestines? Did they get any better?

ME: I'm all right now.

BROTHER: But you mustn't stop the treatment. In your file it says you have diarrhea attacks periodically.

The Brother takes a capsule, just like the one I had hidden in my hand, from a small box. He fills Cortines's mug with water and hands me the mug and the capsule. I already have a capsule in my hand, which makes me hesitant; I won't be able to fool him. He watches me attentively.

BROTHER: Come on now, it won't hurt you.

There's no way out except to take the pill. If it's poison it must be slow-acting and cumulative, otherwise they wouldn't give me several capsules to take. Just one wouldn't kill me.

I take the pill before Cortines's frightened eyes.

The Brother leads me to my cubicle.

I know I'm going to lose my meal. But I'm not going to die, for the time being.

———

It was absurd for them to retire me. It all happened so suddenly. I still could have taught for many years. My adolescent students, for the most part, were perfect imbeciles, but there were always a couple in every group that made it worth the effort to prepare and teach the class. I never understood why so few of them took an interest in history. It's true that the majority didn't want to know about anything at all, my colleagues in other disciplines complained about the same apathy. But clearly the fault didn't lie only with the conditioned and depersonalized students. Yesterday I dreamed I was teaching, and in the dream I was talking about what was Good and what was Bad for humanity. I was saying that the Good was Power and the Evil, the Bad, was Weakness; the weak should be helped to perish. But suddenly I was no longer in a classroom, there was a war, in which the old, the sick, were killed and burned in an oven and the smoke from the oven's smokestack was like that of the Eleventh of May Home. A Nietzschean nightmare.

―――――

So far the capsule hasn't harmed me. It also hasn't cured my diarrhea. I want to think logically and impartially. I know that after almost six months here, inactive, lazy, bored, poorly fed, lonely, and melancholy, I must be very careful with my thoughts. The human being needs security, dignity, well-being, and respect, but here there's nothing but misery and degradation. I feel worse than if I were crazy and in a straitjacket, and my thoughts must show the effects of that. I deduce that the capsule did me no harm because it wasn't poison. In that case it must really be diarrhea medicine, and I should have gotten better, which didn't happen. At this moment I'm sitting on the chamber pot, the third time today, and my feces are thin, foul-smelling water. Hey, hey, I tell the pot, careful with the false logic of your reasoning. It is much more correct and simpler to conclude, based on existing evidence, that I can't judge whether or not the capsule is poison with a cumulative effect, as I supposed at first. Worried, I await new data.

―――――

I feel like seeing Pharoux and Cortines. But I'm afraid to leave my cubicle. I didn't have breakfast, but they brought me the afternoon snack. Why?

In the evening the Brother comes with coffee, bread, and the medication. I had noticed that the afternoon coffee tasted warmed over. The Brothers had admitted that coffee was brewed only once, in the morning. But was that really the taste of old coffee? Why did they make a point that I drink it?

When the Brother leaves I spit the coffee and the capsule into the chamber pot, along with the rest of the mug.

I will not let them poison me.

Tonight I am not overpowered, as always happens, by a turbulent drowsiness. I am already lying down, watching the damned television for over two hours, and sleep doesn't come. The strange taste in the evening coffee is some narcotic, I conclude excitedly. I haven't felt this good for a long time. I am defeating the Brothers!

I need to talk with Pharoux, with Cortines. They can help me. At night the surveillance must be less; they probably think we're all torpid in our beds.

I sneak through the corridor, carrying the full chamber pot. If I'm caught I'll say I'm taking the pot to empty it in the large drain at the end of the corridor. I pass the cubicle once occupied by Baldomero. Since the cubicles have no doors, I see immediately, lying in the bed and illuminated by the weak yellowish bulb in the ceiling and by the blue reflection of the TV, a thin man with long, sparse white hair. When he sees me he rises from the bed, his body shaking, and begins a grotesque dance: he stamps his feet on the floor, waves his arms, and whinnies as if he were a horse.

I am afraid the noise will attract the Brothers. I cover the old man's mouth with my hands. He quiets down docilely and rubs his gums on my hands, sucks my fingers. His saliva is thick and fetid. I feel disgust, wipe my hands on the wall. He emits squeaky little sounds, as if he were a muted horn, and continues to dance, though less noisily.

"I suffer from a rare disease," he says. "My name is Caio, but you can call me Dancer, that's how they all know me."

My senile mind is playing tricks on me; I had almost forgotten Pharoux. I put Dancer in bed, tell him to keep quiet, to play his little horn very softly. He gives the impression that he's crying, but I'm used to old men's sobs and I have things to do.

The corridors are empty. Even so, I walk cautiously until I reach Pharoux's cubicle.

Pharoux is sleeping with his mouth open. His eyepatch has slipped off and in the empty socket is dark red tissue, like the scab of a wound that hasn't fully healed.

I touch Pharoux's shoulder delicately. "Pharoux, Pharoux," I say close to his hairy and ill-smelling ear. I shake him forcefully. Without waking up, he strikes at me, a glancing blow. It's no use. No doubt about it, he's drugged. The same thing must have happened to Cortines.

I return to my cubicle. I've never felt so good in my life. I even think my diarrhea has stopped. I'm smarter than they are. Now I know why no one lasts longer than six months here. If the inmate doesn't die from humiliation and privation, from despair and loneliness, they kill him with poison. The smokestack! That smell is burning flesh! We're not even worth the food we eat, or a decent burial. I can't restrain my happiness. I feel neither fear nor horror at these atrocious discoveries. I'm alive, I escaped, by my own efforts, from the sordid fate they had planned for me, and this fills me with euphoria. My mind is packed with memories and historic reminiscences of the great men who fought against oppression, iniquity, and obscurantism.

If we unite, all the old people of the world, we can change this situation. We can make up for our physical weakness with cunning. I know how all revolutions were carried out.

I spent the night with these sweet thoughts.

The inmates who want to, and they are few, can spend an hour a day in the courtyard to get some sun. In the courtyard we're closely watched by the Brothers. As soon as they see that inmates are talking on a bench, they approach on some pretext, such as enquiring about our health or to talk about the weather, but their purpose is to find out what we're talking about. Knowing this, I sat down near Pharoux and pretended to doze, turning my body and leaning to one side so the Brother who was in the courtyard wouldn't see my mouth.

"Don't look at me, the Brother is watching us," I tell Pharoux.

Pharoux remains impassive, but I know he has nearly perfect hearing. He can't talk, his face is very visible. To show that he hears me, he opens and closes the hand that is resting on his leg several times at regular intervals.

I tell Pharoux all my suspicions. I talk about going to his cubicle at night and about his state of torpor, about the poisoned capsule and the crematory oven. I ask him not to drink the evening coffee and say that I'll visit him. I would have said more, but Pharoux rises and leaves before I finish. Perhaps he did that to avoid suspicion; I had already said what was essential. Maybe he went to turn me in, another hypothesis. After all, he had been a policeman, trained to defend constituted authority, like a guard dog. I should have sought out Cortines and not Pharoux. To tell the truth, Pharoux frightened me; he gave the impression of being capable of every kind of betrayal and act of evil.

—————

In a state of excitement and happiness I haven't felt for a long time, I wait for night to come.

Where is the old man I used to be? My skin is still dry tissue hanging loosely on my bones, my penis an arid and empty strip of flesh, my sphincter muscles don't work, my memory only records what it wants to, I have no teeth, or hair, or breath, or strength. That's how my body is, but I'm no longer that shameful blubberer, frightened and unhappy, whose greatest desire in life was to eat a piece of chocolate. That old being was imposed upon me by a corrupt and vicious society, by an evil system that forces millions of human beings into a parasitic, marginal, and miserable life. I refuse to accept that monstrous torment. I shall await death in the worthiest manner.

Pharoux is awake in his cubicle, on his feet, nervous.

"You're right. They dope us every night. I told Cortines not to drink the coffee either. Let's see if he's still awake too."

We go to Cortines's cubicle. He's sitting on the bed, flexing his biceps.

"We have to do something," I say.

"That oven is for burning the dead, I'm sure of it," Cortines says.

"And why not the living? The ones who're taking too long to die?" Pharoux says.

For a time we argue angrily about whether or not the Brothers are cremating the still-living bodies of inmates. I defend the position that the oven is used only to cremate the dead. Actually, I'm not convinced of this. It may be that the oven is also for the living, or just for garbage.

"I know what to do," Pharoux says. "A riot. We're no better than prisoners here, and when prisoners want to improve things, they riot; they take a few hostages and really raise a stink."

I like the idea. History teaches that all rights are won by force. Weakness generates oppression. But we're just three old men. No! I must forget I'm old. Again I'm accepting the conditioning they imposed on me.

"We are three human beings!" I shout.

Pharoux tells me to speak more softly. His plan is simple. He knows where the Director's apartment is. The door is easy to open, an old-fashioned lock. The Director will be our hostage and our trump card in the negotiations.

We go out, Pharoux, Cortines, and I, into the dark corridors of the Eleventh of May Home. Pharoux has his steel knife in his hand. His lone eye shines brightly; he is tense but wears the professional air of someone who knows what he's doing. We go into another wing, climb one flight. The Home is calm, but we hear the sound of television sets. We climb a short flight of stairs. It's the Director's tower. We come to a door.

"This is it," Pharoux says.

Pharoux takes a piece of wire from his pocket, kneels down. For a long time he works the wire inside the keyhole. We hear the sound of the bolt moving in the strike plate.

Pharoux smiles. "Let's go in." But the door doesn't open. It must be bolted from inside.

On an impulse I knock at the door, loudly.

Nothing happens.

I knock again.

From inside we hear the Director's voice, irritated.

"What is it?"

"Director, sir," I say with my voice half muffled, "an emergency."

The Director opens the door. Pharoux grabs him, Cortines gets a stranglehold on him. Pharoux pricks the Director's face with the knife, drawing a drop of blood.

"Quiet, you fat pig," Pharoux says.

The Director looks at Pharoux in fear. I think it's the first time in his life he's been afraid.

"Take it easy, please, take it easy," the Director says.

We drag the Director inside.

Cortines ties the Director's hands with the belt from his robe. Pharoux orders him to lie down on the floor.

We're in the living room of the apartment. When we enter the bedroom we get a surprise. A woman is sleeping on the wide double bed. She's young, with long legs and arms, and completely naked. I can't recall the last time I saw a naked woman.

The woman wakes up. She sits up in the bed. She asks who we are.

"Edmundo!" the woman screams. So that's the Director's name.

"Keep quiet and nothing will happen to you," I say.

"We'd better tie her up too," Cortines says.

Cortines ties the girl's arms and legs with strips from the bedsheet. She submits docilely. It's not only old people who get intimidated and remain immobile in the face of threats. If the women struggled with Cortines and me, she might manage to get away. But she supposes we're two crazy old men and that the best strategy is not to resist us.

We leave her in the bed, bound. Cortines takes strips from the sheet to tie up the Director. He's lying on the floor on his back, and Pharoux has the knife against his skin. If he moves, the knife will pierce his neck.

"His name is Edmundo," I tell Pharoux.

"Edmundo the filthy," says Pharoux. I sense that the action has awakened repressed destructive instincts in Pharoux. I see small puncture marks on the Director's neck.

We tie the Director's legs and make new bonds, tying his hands still more.

The Director's apartment has a living room, bedroom, kitchen, and bathroom. There's only one entrance, the door we came through. It's a heavy wooden door; its lock is old, but it has a pair of built-in steel bars. We're safe.

"Just look at his refrigerator," Pharoux says.

Beer, eggs, ham, butter. The refrigerator is full.

Cortines and Pharoux go to the kitchen to fry some eggs.

Now they are eating ham and eggs and drinking beer. The thing old people enjoy most is eating. And Pharoux and Cortines are happy, satisfied, as if the object of our revolt was to eat ham and eggs. Perhaps, stricto sensu, that's right, that the final objective of any revolution is more food for all. But at that moment we were merely raiding the refrigerator of the Director of an old folks' asylum—a Home by official hypocrisy.

I eat only a piece of bread. I would like to caress the woman's body, but she would surely be repulsed and that would put an end to my pleasure.

I begin to feel a great weariness. I lie down on the living room sofa . . . I think I can sleep a little, the negotiations may drag on . . . I have to keep an eye on Pharoux so he won't do anything stupid, he's very violent . . . I feel we're initiating a revolution . . . but it's necessary that our gesture go beyond this tower and cause others to think . . . God, I'm tired! . . . Before going to sleep I must speak with Pharoux and Cortines. They're in the kitchen, eating noisily . . . we have to make our plans . . .

THE BOOK OF PANEGYRICS

One can either see or be seen.
—John Updike, Self-Consciousness

I DON'T FIND THE NEWS I'm looking for in the paper. But the ad for a male nurse—good references, to take care of a sick old man—could be one, temporary, solution to my problem.

A woman opens the apartment door on Delfim Moreira Avenue, and I say I came because of the ad. She tells me to come in. An enormous living room. The windows are open and the very blue sea is visible outside. Big goddamn deal. A man is standing at the window, and he turns around when I come in. He comes toward me.

"It's to take care of my father. Do you have references?"

I don't have references. Over twenty years ago, when I was a boy, I took care of a sick old man, and at his house I read dozens of books and had my sexual initiation with a rubber doll named Gretchen. But all I did was push the wheelchair and clean up the crap. "Yes, I do. Good references," I say.

"Very good." The man looks at his watch. He says how much he'll pay me per month; he asks if I can start today, he'll pay extra. He's leaving on a trip tonight and is in a hurry.

The woman is also in a hurry.

"I didn't bring any clothes," I say.

"One thing that's not lacking in this house is clothes. Open the closets and take what you want. Here, on this paper are the addresses and telephone numbers of my father's attending physician and of our lawyer. If necessary, call the doctor, but nothing's going to happen; my father is healthy as an ox. Any other problems, money or whatever, speak with the lawyer. Here's the numbers of the pharmacy and the supermarket; all you have to do is call, have them deliver, and sign for the bills. On this other sheet is what you have to do as nurse. It's not very complicated. Every three days you have a day off; a nurse will take your place. Then you can go home and pick up your clothes. Well, I think that takes care of everything. Any questions?"

"No." I want to get rid of him as badly as he wants to get rid of the old man.

"Ah, I almost forgot. My father's name is Baglioni. Mr. Baglioni. Let's go to his room."

We go down a long corridor to the old man's room. He's lying on a bed.

"Dad, this is your new friend— What is your name?"

"José."

"José. He's going to take care of you."

The old man has white hair. He looks at me. He complains that he doesn't like to have people come into his room when he isn't wearing his dentures.

"He's not just anybody, Dad, he's José."

The old man puts in his dentures. He looks at me. The man leans over and kisses the old man on the forehead. The woman does the same.

At the door the man gives me a wad of bills. "Three months in advance. Plus the bonus. Any questions?"

"No."

The woman sighs. They both look at their watches. They forgot to ask for my references. They don't want to waste any more time; they're traveling and must be late. I go to the door with them.

"This key is to the door. The red one is to the safe. The medicine is in the safe."

They leave.

I read the instructions. The safe—heavy, square, made of polished steel—is in the pantry. I open the safe; all I see in it is medicine. I look around the various rooms in the house. I open the closets. All the windows are barred. These people live on the third floor and have bars on the windows. Afraid of Spider-Man. The walls of one room are taken up by shelves that are filled to the ceiling with books. Big goddamn deal. The old man's house in Flamengo was crammed with so many books that it made my head spin, but that was back then; I was a kid. The kitchen is spacious, with an enormous electric stove, microwave, blenders, juicers, refrigerators and freezers full of labeled plastic boxes, and cupboards bulging with cans and boxes of food. But, according to the instructions, the old man has vegetable soup and a bit of gelatin for dinner. Besides the food, which is ready in the freezer, I'm supposed to give him a Pankreoflat pill, a Ticlid, and Lexotan, six milligrams. I know what Lexotan is used for; since there are lots of boxes of it in the cupboard, I'll take one from time to time. Ticlid. I open the box and read the instruction sheet. I really enjoy reading medical instruction sheets. Ticlid is "a powerful antithrombin containing as its active component a new and original substance, ticlopine hydrochloride. Indicated in cases that require a reduction of the concentration and adhesion level of platelets." Pankreoflat has "as active components Pancreatina triplex and dimethylpolysylloxan which have been rendered highly active through a special process."

Eight o'clock. I had already warmed up the soup. I take the old man out of the bed and set him in the armchair.

"It's time for your soup."

"I don't want any soup." He has all his teeth in, uppers and lowers.

"Then eat the gelatin."

"I don't want any gelatin."

If he doesn't want it, he doesn't want it, fine. But I force him to take the medicines. He must be nervous on our first day, but the Lexotan will lower his tension and anxiety level.

I lift the old man from the chair easily. Instead of feeling happy in my arms, he looks at me as if he hates me. In bed, following instructions, I put a disposable diaper on him; he tries to stop me, but he's weak and his resistance is very minimal.

"Do you know who I am?" he asks.

"Yes, I do, Mr. Baglioni, don't worry."

I pull on the cord with the button that rings the bell and put it beside the bed, next to the TV remote control, as instructed.

"If you want anything, ring the bell."

I put the dishes in the dishwasher. I get ham from the refrigerator and make a sandwich.

My room is comfortable, with a small bathroom, a television, and a bookcase. If it were the old days, I would examine it book by book, to see if any of them interested me, but I don't even look at the bookcase. The newscast on TV doesn't give me the news I'm interested in. The old man doesn't call me during the night; the Lexotan must be doing its job.

I watch the final newscast of the evening. Nothing.

I walk around the house. I go into the library but don't read any of the books. I take one of the old man's Lexotans, but even then I can't get to sleep. I'm a tough case.

At 7 A.M. I go to see the old man. He's already awake. I follow the instructions. First I rinse his eyes with boric acid. Then I remove the diaper, which is dirty from shit and urine. I clean the old man with a sponge, feeling tremendous disgust. I dress him in pajamas.

"I'm going to bring your tea and toast."

A newspaper had been stuck under the kitchen door. I open the newspaper but don't find the item I was looking for.

I put a little milk in the tea. He drinks a cup and eats a piece of toast. I give him an Adalat, "20 mg of nifedipine," and another of Tagamet, "carboxymethyl-amido-hydroxipropyl-methyl-cellulose." Next I transfer the old man from the bed to the armchair and turn on the television. Cartoons. "If you want anything, ring the bell."

I re-read the newspaper. Nothing. I pick up the phone. It's necessary to be careful. I go back to the old man's room. There's an extension on his night table. I pretend to be straightening up the table and pull the phone cord out of the wall. The old man looks at me pensively; maybe he realizes what I did.

I make the call from the living room. No one answers. I over-hear a cross-connection. "They put ground glass in my borscht." I hang up, concerned. Cross-connections make me nervous. Ground glass in the borscht? Some code? Smart people talk in code on the phone. I should have kept on listening. I try again and no one answers.

I hear the old man's bell.

"I have a proposal," he says.

Whenever anyone has made me a proposal, it's always been no big goddamn deal. "I can't listen to any of your proposals."

"Open that closet," the old man says.

The closet is full of boxes of cigars, Cuban, American, Jamaican, Dutch, Brazilian. "I don't smoke," I tell him.

"There's a box of Empire cigars, isn't there? A large box. Open the box."

The box is full of cigars, as large and thick as a policeman's billy club.

"Well?" says the old man.

"I don't smoke. And if I did smoke, I wouldn't smoke one of those."

"Not that box, the other one."

The other box is full of hundred-real bills. Big goddamn deal.

"I'm not interested in any kind of proposal," I tell him. I put the box in its place and close the closet door.

The old man tries to grab my arm. "Listen, you imbecile," he says.

"I'm very sorry. If you want anything, ring the bell."

I make a phone call from the living room again. The one I want doesn't answer.

"They put ground glass in my Porsche." It's the cross-connection. Porsche? Borscht? Damned code. Borscht? I hang up.

Lunchtime. Soup and papaya, taken from the freezer. Ticlid and Pankreoflat.

"You'll never be anything in life," he says.

I take care of the old man for three days and nights. He talks more all the time.

"Do you know when I discovered I was old? When my pubic hair began to fall out and more hair started growing in my nose." He tells me while I'm sponging his balls.

No one answers the phone calls I make. After the third cross-connection, I stop calling. Neither the newspapers nor television have the news I'm waiting for.

On the fourth day a nurse comes to relieve me. We're more or less the same age.

"So Van disappeared?" she says.

"What Van?"

"Vanderley, the male nurse."

"I don't know anything about that."

"When Van disappeared they wanted me to come and take over, but I told them I couldn't leave my shift at the hospital. They know I work at the hospital."

The apartment has another bedroom just for her. She goes into her bedroom and comes out a short time later dressed in a clean white uniform, with a white cap, white shoes, and white stockings. A pleasant perfume comes from her body.

"Is Mr. Baglioni all right?"

"Yes."

"Where did you go to school?"

"That's none of your business," I reply.

"Try to get here on time tomorrow. I have to be at the hospital at nine."

"Don't worry."

"Van was always late."

"I'm never late."

"Are those your clothes?"

The shirt and pants I'm wearing are too short. I got them out of a closet somewhere in the house.

"The guy told me to get whatever clothes I wanted. I didn't have time to go home. Van's the one to blame, for disappearing."

"My name is Lou."

"Lou?"

"Lourdes. What's yours?"

"José." I remembered the old man in Flamengo and his wheelchair. "Why isn't there a wheelchair here?"

"Mr. Baglioni's son doesn't want one."

"Why are the medicines in the safe?"

"So Mr. Baglioni can't kill himself."

"He can't even walk by himself."

"Before he broke his femur he could."

"So the bars on the windows."

"That was a long time ago, when he made the first attempt."

I leave. I look for the doorman. "I work for Mr. Baglioni, on the third floor. Where's the telephone switch box?"

"What for?"

"The phone's got something wrong with it and I want to take a look."

"Are you a repairman?"

"Just show me where the box is."

He takes me to a wooden door. "Here it is. But I don't have the key."

"You better get one right now or I'll break this piece of shit down."

He knows I'm not kidding. People always know when I'm not kidding. He gives me the key.

"You can go; I'll close it behind me."

It's easy to identify the wires to Mr. Baglioni's apartment. The building has only one apartment per floor. None of the phone lines are tapped at the box. But there are other places where it can be done. It's a fucker.

I return the key to the doorman. I get a taxi. I'm carrying the wad of money they gave me in my pocket. The other pocket is heavy with telephone tokens. I've decided on the hotel I'm going to, one on Buarque de Macedo Street, in the Flamengo district. I've never been there. I never stay twice at the same hotel. On the way I buy a small suitcase, six pairs of undershorts, six shirts, a pair of pants, shaving cream, and razor blades.

A mediocre hotel, with no telephone in the room, but that doesn't bother me. A phone in the room is dangerous; the switchboard operator amuses herself by listening to the guests' conversations. I close the room's curtains and lie down, after taking off my shoes. I spend the day lying in bed.

At night I go out, to call from a pay phone. Nobody answers. I buy a cheese sandwich and a can of Coca-Cola and go back to the hotel. I sit down on the only chair in the room. I'm waiting to feel hungry and eat the sandwich and drink the Coca-Cola.

Daylight starts coming in through the gaps in the curtain. I take a bath and shave. I pay the hotel and leave. I get a taxi.

I try to open the old man's apartment and can't. A bolt is holding the door from the inside. I ring the bell. Lou opens the apartment door. Lou's uniform doesn't have a single wrinkle. Either she was on her feet all night or she just put on a fresh uniform. I smell the perfume, from the uniform and from her body.

"I've already given him the milk, the Adalat, and the Tagamet. I bathed him, perfumed him, shaved him, and cut his nose hair. You didn't perfume him."

"It's not in the instruction the guy gave me."

"You have to cut his nose hair. The hairs grow fast, and he doesn't like hairs in his nose."

"It's not in the instructions."

"In the evening you didn't give him his milk with Meritene. And don't forget the Seloken."

It's in the instructions. Seloken, an inhibitor of the adrenergic receptors located mainly in the heart. "I missed it. How did you know I didn't give it to him?"

"I just know."

She goes into her room, changes clothes. Jeans, sneakers, a T-shirt, handbag on her shoulder.

"Where's your uniform?"

"I told the guy I wasn't going to wear a uniform. Look, don't butt into my life."

"It's unhygienic to work without a uniform. Another thing. Did you pull out the telephone wire in the bedroom?"

"Yes. What's that phone good for? All it does it disturb the old man."

"You may be right," she said, before leaving.

"Good morning," I tell the old man in his armchair. He's wearing striped pajamas. I smell the perfume.

"There is a plant in the Namibian desert that lives a thousand years on nothing but the morning dew," he says.

Big goddamn deal. I turn on the television. "If you want anything, ring the bell."

I call from the living room. Nobody answers. This time there's no cross-connection, or they're keeping quiet, to hear what the others are saying.

The bell rings.

"Yes?"

"Turn off the television and put me in bed. I'm tired."

He's stretched out in bed, his legs crossed.

"Open the drawer. Get the book that's in it."

The hard-bound book has his picture on the cover. He looks twenty years younger.

"Isn't liking books as much as women a terrible sign?"

I give him the book. "If you want anything, ring the bell."

"Wait. You know when I discovered I was old? When I started to enjoy eating more than fucking. That's a terrible sign, worse than hair growing in your nose. Now I don't even enjoy eating," he says.

"I don't enjoy eating either. If you want anything, ring the bell."

"Read this book," he says.

I pick up the book with his picture on the cover. "If you want anything, ring the bell," I repeat.

I read the book in my room. It's a series of testimonials from friends, professional colleagues about the old man—important people saying what a great man he was. They all say the same thing about intelligence, generosity, culture, Baglioni's public spirit.

At lunchtime the old man doesn't speak to me about the book. In the afternoon I give him the Meritene with milk. At dinner he asks me if I read the book.

"Yes."

"Well?"

"Well what?"

"I want your opinion."

"I thought it was a piece of shit. A pile of stupidity."

"I was going to die and my friends decided to publish the book. It was my fault." He took out his teeth. He was already taking liberties with me. "I'm sleepy. Remind me later to talk about that. Don't forget. I want to talk to you about it."

I put him into the bed. Stretched out with his legs crossed.

I call from the living room phone. Finally, they answer.

"It's me," I say.

"Where'd you get to?"

"I can't say. Look—"

"They follow the lightning's flash." Holy shit, it's the cross-connection.

"There's a cross-connection. I'm going to hang up."

"Tell me where you are and I'll call you back. I'm going to have to go out."

"They're waiting for the rainbow." Goddamn cross-connection.

"Let me call you." I hang up the phone and go to the old man's room. He's sleeping. He's not going to wake up if I go out for ten minutes.

I call from a pay phone in the street. It rings and no one answers.

I'm back in my room.

Is it really a cross-connection? The words are in code. The lightning-flash voice seemed to be the same as borscht Porsche bosch, but maybe it wasn't. Well, I wasn't in any hurry. No one knows where I am. I take one of the old man's Lexotans.

The next day, after cleaning the old man's parts and rinsing his eyes with boric acid, and after giving him tea with milk and toast, the Adalat, and the Tagamet:

"Can you imagine how it feels to plan to publish a book of panegyrics after your death and end up not dying?"

"What's the problem?"

"As I lay in my death throes, a hasty friend distributed two-thousand copies of the book, which they hadn't showed me because I was dying, saying what a great loss my death was and showering me with praise. Even if the book were good, which it isn't, I would have to be embarrassed. I didn't die, understand?"

"I understand. Were you really the greatest lawyer in Brazil?"

"That's another of the book's idiocies. Nobody's the greatest anything. I was a lawyer who knew how to make a lot of money, at a time when economists hadn't yet taken power."

"There are worse things than having an idiotic book written about you."

"Yes, yes, so there are. For example, your sperm becoming as thin as water. But I can't help but remember that ridiculous book. Over half of the books ended up in used-book stores. I sent a friend to buy all of them back, which cost me next to nothing; they were gathering dust. I destroyed every one I could get my hands on. But there are others out there somewhere."

He was short of breath.

"You can tell me the rest later."

"You're going to listen, aren't you? You strike me as an intelligent sort. For a male nurse."

"Tomorrow. Rest now."

After breakfast, after lunch, and before dinner, always on those occasions, he sits me down to talk about his life. He wanders a bit, but it's easy enough to follow what he says; a bit of rearranging:

The headaches arose overnight. They were so strong that the usual analgesics offered no relief. The doctors who examined him made their diagnoses and suggested that he get other opinions. They confirmed the illness abroad. The old man had six months to live, maybe a little more, maybe a little less.

His greatest fear was always to die suddenly, without being able to tear up the papers that had to be destroyed, without rewarding those who should be rewarded or punishing those who should be punished, without being able to dispose of his goods in a way he considered fair. Knowing that he had six months to live was a kind of consolation. He made his confession to a priest who was a friend and was absolved of his sins. He professed a good and compassionate religion that offered salvation to all right up to the last moment. He'd always had a great capacity for suffering humiliation, for accepting insults, for confronting and overcoming obstacles. After he had his revenge on those who had offended him, in the fullest and most absolute way, and he always had his revenge, he would afford himself the luxury of forgiving. Forgiveness after vengeance. So, retaliation occupied an important spot among his last acts of will. Yes, revenge was a sin, but at the last moment he would repent and be pardoned. The priest had told him that there was no exact time for repentance to enter the hearts of men, so long as it was real. The old man knew he would genuinely repent after annihilating his enemies and that he would die redeemed, ready to face whatever came after death.

The year before his diagnosis, he had been named Man of the Year by an important weekly magazine, and he had confided in his old friend Sampaio, with whom he had founded the largest law firm in the country, that he'd like to stop and write his biography. He was starting to feel old, and he would like to be remembered by posterity. Sampaio had said that could wait; there was a lot to do at the firm. And he'd added, no doubt correctly, that the old man's life wouldn't interest others—he didn't have enough material for a biography. This Sampaio guy knew that there are lots of people who think their life is interesting but it's not. Others think their life is shit and it is.

Lou arrives when the old man is sitting in the armchair talking about his life. I didn't bolt the door, so when she comes in she catches us talking. When he sees her, the old man's face lights up. He seems torn between having her company or mine, now that I've become a kind of confidant. Lou says she's going to put on her uniform. I go after her.

"What has Mr. Baglioni so worked up?"

"His life."

"Really? How about that."

She goes into her bedroom.

She comes out gleaming, all starched and perfumed.

"I'm going to take a bath," I say.

She's standing at the door to my room when I come out.

"Did you take some Lexotan?"

"Yes."

"Hmm."

"I'm going to make a phone call before I leave."

This time the phone only rings twice before someone answers. It's a strange voice.

"Who's this?" I ask.

"Who do you want to talk to?"

My ear throbs. It throbs whenever I sense I'm in danger. I hang up the phone, not knowing what to do.

"Do you mind if I sleep here today, during your shift?"

"As long as you don't interfere with my work . . ." she says.

I stay in my room, lying down. It's getting more dangerous all the time out there.

Lou knocks at the door. "You want anything for dinner?" she asks from outside. The day went by quickly.

"No, thanks," I shout from inside.

"I'll bring it to you."

"I'm not hungry. Thanks."

Lou knocks on the door. "You want anything for breakfast?" The night went by quickly. "I'm coming," I shout.

"You slept in your clothes?" Lou asks at the breakfast table.

"I don't have any pajamas."

"Or a uniform."

"Are you married?"

"Why do you want to know?"

"I was thinking about your husband."

"I don't have a husband."

"A lucky guy. The one who didn't marry you."

"Very funny. And you, are you married?"

"I used to be married to Gretchen."

Lou pats her hair under her nurse's cap.

There are lots of things on the table. I have tea with milk and toast.

"Are you on the same diet as Mr. Baglioni?"

"I don't feel hungry in the morning."

"You're very thin. They're going to think you have AIDS."

"I do."

"That isn't funny."

"Thanks for the tea." I feel like asking what perfume she is wearing, but I leave the table. The old man's bell rings.

He is shaved, washed, and perfumed. "Has the girl left?"

"She's finishing her breakfast."

"When she leaves, come back here. We have to talk."

———

Sampaio was right. The old man was incapable of writing his own biography. He'd been married to three jealous women and been afraid of them all, more of the first than the second, and a little less of the last one. Lunchtime was the perfect time for him to make his getaway without arousing any suspicion in the wife he was married to at the time; at least twice a week, for over thirty years, he would make up some business lunch and tell his secretary about it, so he could hop into bed with another woman.

His last wife was the calmest of all. He had always married poor women. At the time of the first marriage he was poor himself, but by the second he was already a very rich man, and his wife was a crafty and unscrupulous young woman from the outskirts. There are men who can't be humiliated, not because they don't feel the humiliation but because they consider themselves above it. So, the embarrassment to which his second wife subjected him had been administered coldly. He would lie beside her at night, thinking of how to make her go back to the petit bourgeois ostracism from which he had taken her. He pretended, up to a certain point, to know nothing about his wife's lovers, and he even enjoyed himself with the last one, a gigolo who claimed to be a metopomanist and went by the, probably false, name José de Arimathea.

"Metopomanist? What the shit is that?" I ask.

The old man knows why he remembers that guy, out of the several of his second wife's lovers that he knew about. Arimathea told him on the day they met—at a dinner at his house, which his second wife had organized to present the guy to high society—that he wasn't a card reader, a palm reader, or a charlatan, but rather a scientist who could judge someone's character, and make predictions about their future, by studying the lines on their forehead; theasome erroneously called that science metoposcopy, which besides being etymologically incorrect, recalled dactyloscopy, endoscopy, and other less transcendental oscopies. And Arimathea had asked him if he, the old man, knew why women were more mysterious than men.

"Know what the charlatan told me? That women are more mysterious than men because they hide the wrinkles in their faces. And the cretin actually taught me a lesson. Until we got married I never saw my second wife without makeup, the same makeup she was wearing when she was chosen Miss Nova Iguaçu Country Club and which she thought gave her the subtle, porcelain-like look of an exotic Japanese theater actress."

In the middle of the story the old man has an asthma attack. I get the Berotex Spray and spray it into his mouth. Since the attack doesn't go away, I stick two suppositories of children's Eufilin in his ass. It's in the instructions. Lou explained to me that there used to be an Euphyllin with 'ph' and two 'l's, a bronchodilator for adults, but they did away with that medicine and made Eufilin, with simplified spelling for children; but children and old people are the same thing.

"I'm going to rest a bit now. If you want anything, ring the bell." I leave the old man on the bed, on his back with his legs crossed.

Lou is wearing her other uniform, the one for the street: jeans, sneakers, T-shirt, a bag on her shoulder. I wait for her to leave and go to the old man's room. He's still in the same position, his legs crossed. I open the closet, get the cigar box. The money is there.

"Change your mind?" the old man asks.

"No. I came to see if the money was still here."

"She's honest. Treat her well. I need her more than I need you." The old man's voice still isn't back to normal.

"Rest a while longer."

"I want to go to the library."

"After lunch."

"I want to go now."

"I follow instructions."

"To hell with instructions."

"If you want anything, ring the bell."

I need to make a phone call, but it can't be from the house. They'll end up discovering where I'm calling from. It has to be from a public phone, but I can't leave now, with the old man recovering from an asthma attack.

I pace around the house. The bell rings.

"I don't want to be alone," the old man says.

I sit on the sofa in the bedroom. "I'll stay here, but you be quiet, all right?" He shuts his eyes. He opens his eyes, looks at me. He closes his eyes. Opens. Closes. Sleeps. When he's sleeping, he reminds me of an old dog I had when I was a child.

I stretch out on the sofa. I smell Lou's scent; she must lie there during the night, watching over the old man, like a good nurse. How is it that her uniform never has a single crease, a fold, a small wrinkle?

After lunch I pick up the old man and carry him to the library. I ought to make the old man walk there, but he's afraid of putting any weight on the leg he broke; a metal prosthesis was inserted into his leg, and as a result he walks disjointedly, limping, looking like he could fall at any moment. In the library there's a large armchair where I make the old man comfortable. I turn on the floor lamp beside the chair.

"Get the Macauley, with the red cover," he says. "These days I only enjoy reading the old historians. Burckhardt, Gibbon, Mommsen. I read without glasses, did you know that?"

I find the book. I take it out of the bookcase and hand it to him.

"Can you manage to read that small print?"

The book is in English. "Yes."

"Then read."

"*He was still in his novitiate of infamy*," I read.

"You read English?"

Big goddamn deal. "I'm a good nurse," I say, but he doesn't catch the irony.

"Macauley is speaking of Barère."

"Can I go out for a little bit?"

"It's not in the instructions," says the old man. "I'm joking. You may go."

"Five minutes."

I check that the safe with the medicine is securely locked; you can never be too careful. I leave. I call from a pay phone.

"Where are you?"

"That's not important," I say.

"I need to talk to you."

"So talk."

"You said it was dangerous to talk on the phone."

"I'm on a pay phone."

"It's still dangerous. Let's meet."

"I'll think about it. I'll call you later."

"Later might be too late."

I hang up.

I buy a newspaper. Nothing. I throw the paper in a trash can.

The old man has fallen on the floor, in the middle of several books.

"I tried to get the Burckhardt from the shelf and fell. This book here." He shows me the book he has in his hands.

I sit the old man down in the armchair. He gives me the book. "I want you to read me a passage from this book."

I open the book. "I don't read German."

"Ah, ah," he says. "I'll read it for you."

He translates as he reads, without hesitation. It's the story of a general and the inhabitants of a city that the general liberated from the enemy. Every day they would meet to see how they could reward the general, but they could never find a compensation worthy of the great favor he had done them. Finally, one of them had an idea–kill the general and then worship him as the patron saint of the city. Which is what they did.

"Did you understand it?"

Big goddamn deal. I stopped thinking books were important a long time ago.

"I find your life more interesting."

"Really?" He throws the book on the floor and happily resumes his story.

The metopomanist had taught him a lesson. So when he met his future third wife, the first thing the old man asked her to do was wash her face. And behind the makeup, because this woman also used makeup perfectly, he discovered traces of melancholy, sadness, and death, which made him like her more than the others. But he continued having affairs; it was much more exciting when he was married. Maybe that's why he had married early and was a bachelor between wives so briefly.

The more money he made, the more power he exercised, the greater his desire for women. He celebrated, by fucking, his nominations to the lower courts and to the high court, the influence that he exercised in the elections of every type that he manipulated, even for run-of-the-mill races like the academies of letters and medicine. One day, in February, a month after turning sixty-nine, upon managing the nomination of an idiot minister who almost brought down the government, he preferred going to lunch with a lawyer from the office, breaking an appointment with a beautiful woman that he had taken great pains to seduce. For some time he had liked eating and drinking in ever larger amounts; he tried, fruitlessly, to stop the growth of his waist by drinking herbal teas, taking homeopathic pills, and having daily massages

in the morning before he left for the office. The flaccid protuber-
ance of his belly; his large, square butt; his sagging breasts which,
if not covered by hair would resemble an old woman's; and the
penis that had become thin, long, and soft, more and more like a
frozen, empty piece of gut, all this had demanded a certain cau-
tion in amorous encounters for some time. He avoided rooms with
mirrors, especially ones with mirrors on the ceiling; when women
fornicate in rooms with mirrors on the ceiling they become mes-
merized by the reflection of their own body, but at certain moments they also look at their companion's. So the lights should be
turned out; half-shadow was the maximum brightness acceptable
in the room. In the act of taking off and putting on clothes there
was a sense of propriety to be obeyed, a right moment for taking
off the shirt, the pants, the shorts, for getting into and out of
bed; the right distance between him and his partner had to be
rigorously established, the closer the better. And after sex it was
necessary to prevent the woman from seeing that his come was
as thin and watery as skim milk. It was necessary to have the
bathtub ready and take the woman there immediately and wash
her pussy, pretending that this was an act of submissive affection.
Fucking demanded rigorous staging, an exhausting theatrical
performance. Not to mention the problems of various kinds that
any woman who goes to bed with a man creates for him.

One hot, humid February, instead of looking for new women,
he started thinking about those he'd already had; or imagin-
ing, just fantasizing, how it would be to copulate with the pretty
women he met at social dinners, without, however, getting involved with them, satisfying himself merely with seductive but
innocuous conversation.

"I always wanted to die slowly, without haste. My greatest fear
in life was always that I'd die suddenly and not be able to orga-
nize my life."

"You told me that. You're repeating yourself. I think it's best
to rest a bit."

I pick up the old man and carry him to the bedroom. I give
him two Lexotans. While I wait for the old man to fall asleep, I

imagine I'm him. I stick my finger in my nose, but I don't feel any hairs in the nostrils. I don't see hairs coming out of his nose; Lou must have cut them. I need to have a look at my come.

Time is passing, I have to act, do something. It can't be by phone; it might be tapped. If I could only decipher those codes; ground glass in the borscht, guys orienting themselves by the thunder, what the shit could that be?

The old man is sleeping. I check the safe. I leave for the street. I call from the pay phone.

"We need to see each other."

"Not yet," I say. "They put ground glass in my borscht." I wait for a reaction from the other end.

Silence.

"They orient themselves by the thunder."

"I don't understand."

"By the flash of lightning."

"I still don't understand. We need to see each other."

I hang up.

The next day the old man wakes up groggy, haggard, listless. Two Lexotans at once is too much for him. He isn't hungry, and he doesn't tell me the story of his life.

Lou arrives. She asks what's wrong with the old man. I don't mention the two Lexotans.

I like the perfume of her body. When Lou laughs, a little of her gum shows, pink and healthy flesh. Looked at without preconception, she's pretty. But today, taking away the perfume, she doesn't look well, and it's not just worry over the old man. Something happened with her. While she goes to take care of the old man, I prepare coffee for the two of us. I know that Lou likes toast with raspberry jam and coffee with cream.

"Let's bury the hatchet," I say.

Lou pensively takes a small sip from her cup. "I'm not fighting with you."

"I made the toast you like, with raspberry."

"Thank you," she says, trying to smile. She merely nibbles the toast.

I tell her I'm also going to stay home today. She repeats that it doesn't bother her. I go to my room.

At lunchtime I ask how the old man is, and Lou answers that he's all right now.

I spend the day in my room and go out only twice, to get something to eat. Once I catch her crying but pretend I didn't see anything.

In the morning she's still unhappy, and I feel like hugging and kissing her. Lou leaves before I can offer her a word of encouragement.

The old man, as always after being taken care of by Lou, is alert, clean, and fragrant.

"Sit there and listen," the old man says.

At the time he thought he was about to buy it, he was in great pain. The doctors injected him with morphine. It was good to get morphine. The pain went away and he was thirty years old again and plunging into the calm waters of a beach in the Northeast, protected by reefs that calmed and heated the waves. As he floated in these warm, salty waters, scenes of women he'd had came into his mind—the other women, not his wives, which he remembered as if he were in a theater. Solange, sitting on the low dresser in the apartment on Athénée Square, her legs folded under her so that her feet could also rest on the furniture, her in front of him, their heads at the same level, and his penis, without needing to be guided by his hand or hers, found its tepid groove. Sara, whom he awaited nude, walking back and forth in the apartment, and when she arrived he would furiously tear off the clothes she was wearing and start to possess her standing up, in the foyer. Sonia, in the launch beyond the bar during a storm, both of them thinking they would be swallowed by the waters while they screwed in the rocking cabin. Silvia, his first wife's best friend, fucking him in the living room while his wife took a bath upstairs. The morphine made him recall the women in groups of names beginning with the same letter. Another day there was Martha, Myrthes, Miriam. Later, Heloisa, Helga, Hilda. He had fucked every letter of the alphabet.

He no longer feels any pleasure at recalling his libidinous feats. All that remains is a happiness, which could be called erotic, but which he prefers to consider aesthetic. But he doesn't tell me that; I'll find that out later.

"But I didn't die. Understand? I got even with my wives, my enemies, at least some of them, and by an ironic twist of fate ended up punishing myself with that grotesque book of encomiums, suffering an even greater chastisement than I had inflicted on others."

He had been invited to, and had agreed to participate in, all the grand parties that took place in the country, all the presidential inauguration banquets, all the luxurious free feeds; he had appeared at least once a week in the society columns of the major newspapers in Rio de Janeiro and São Paulo. Some idiot had detailed it all in the book of panegyrics. Another one wrote of the trips he had taken. About kissing the Pope's ring. All those big goddamn deals.

"I'll pass into history as a ridiculous *arriviste*."

"How did you get even with your wives?"

"With one, by watching with pleasure as she died of cancer. Another, by having her killed. She'd been Miss Guadalupe Country Club."

"You said before that she'd been Miss Nova Iguaçu."

"Guadalupe. When she had access to free caviar she'd eat like a pig, knowing it would give her intense diarrhea. She lied even when she said she'd read *The Little Prince*. Do you think I'm a monster?"

"I don't know."

"One day I came home unexpectedly and found her in bed with a guy who she said was teaching her art history. I let it pass. But when the tennis instructor slapped her on the court at the country club, out of jealousy over another lover, that was too much. It's easy to have a person killed when you have power and money. Easier still if you're somebody like me with cardinals, condottieri, artists, and mafiosi in your genealogy. Have you heard of the Baglioni, of Perugia? Fifteenth century, Italy. They're my ancestors. They're in Burckhardt."

Big goddamn deal. "No. What about the third one? The one who didn't use makeup and you knew from the lines on her face that she was a good person."

"She killed herself. I don't want to talk about that. It was my fault. There are sins so great they can only be punished by absolution."

"And you feel forgiven."

"Unfortunately."

"I can see you're suffering from that forgiveness."

"I suffer more from that indestructible book of adulation."

Then he repeats again that he bought up all the books he could find and destroyed them, but many, scattered throughout Brazil and the world, survived and he talks about the embarrassment and all that.

He's very tired.

"I think it's best to rest a bit."

"Yes, we'll continue later."

I lie down on the sofa, to keep an eye on the old man, but also to smell Lou's perfume. I sleep and dream about her. I stick my hand between the buttons of her immaculate white nurse's blouse and caress her small breast. That's the entire dream.

In the morning, when I give the old man a sponge bath, I think about Lou. Today is the day she comes. The old man confides in me again, and I listen to the acts of infamy he has committed, his boasting ("I screwed the mother and the daughter"), his maxims ("happily married women make the best lovers," "power increases sexual desire," "a man should lose his teeth while still young so that the loss doesn't interfere with his libido"). He refers for the hundredth time to the frustration he felt at preparing to die and not dying.

"The doctors told me I could relax because I still had six months to live. I could prepare to die and I did prepare. Those idiot doctors only discovered later that I had a disease that would make me an invalid but wouldn't kill me. I'm never going to die."

"You already told me that."

I want Lou to show up right away; dreaming about her left me anxious. I have no patience for the old man's stories. I like him; it's just that I have very little patience right now.

Lou arrives in her street uniform: jeans, white T-shirt, handbag on her shoulder, sneakers. She's still sad. She goes into her room. She reappears in her impeccable uniform. I'm going to tell her I dreamed about her and that in the dream I stuck my hand inside her blouse and caressed her breast. But because she still has a sad look on her face, I say instead: "Are you unhappy? What happened?"

"My boyfriend left me."

Maybe she expects me to say something, but I remain silent.

"He left me for another woman."

Since I don't say anything, she heads for the old man's bedroom.

The newspapers don't have the news that concerns me, and I shouldn't make phone calls because they might find out my address. The best thing would be to sleep in the old man's apartment, but I think it's better not to stay by myself with a woman who's been cast aside; that's cowardice. I tell Lou I'll be back before nine. As always, I go to a different hotel, the Apa this time, on Barata Ribeiro Street. As always, I use my false identification card. In the room, I take off my shoes and lie down on the bed. I think about Lou. I wasn't able to tell her I'd dreamed about her; saying that to an abandoned woman is playing dirty. At night I go out. Standing up, in a nearby bar, I eat a cheese sandwich and drink a beer.

I sleep sitting up in the hotel room and dream about Lou again, but this time it's a nightmare. We're in bed and she changes into Gretchen and escapes from my embrace like one of those inflatable balls when it's punctured. She even makes that little sound of air escaping through the hole.

As always, the old man's apartment door is locked from the inside and I have to ring the bell for Lou to open the door.

The old man is acting strange, but I don't ask him to explain what that means. I smell her perfume. She tells me that it's her turn to prepare my breakfast today, but she doesn't know what I like.

"Just coffee is fine."

Lou doesn't seem as depressed. She's still unhappy, but she seems to have made a decision, which always makes people stronger.

She observes me over breakfast.

"You were never a nurse. I know."

It's not a criticism. It's curiosity.

"A long time ago I took care of an old man in Flamengo Beach. While the old man was dying I used to pass the days reading the books in his library and the nights making love to a plastic doll."

"A plastic doll? How sad."

"I was a kid."

"Did you like her? The doll?"

"I was a lonely kid. With Gretchen I could talk."

"What happened to her?"

"She got punctured. They found me another one, called Claudia."

"Another plastic doll?"

"Yes."

"What happened to her?"

"I stopped being a child. I got tired of playing with dolls."

"You're not playing with me, are you?"

"No."

"And today? What do you really do?"

The bell from the old man's room interrupted our conversation.

"The old man is calling. See you Wednesday," I say, sending her on her way.

I go to see the old man.

"Has the girl left?"

"She's on her way now."

"Had you ever met a killer before?"

"Yes."

"And did you despise them? Or hate them? Fear them?"

"No."

"Have you ever killed anyone?"

"Yes."

"What did you feel?"

"How about you? What did you feel, when you killed your wife?"

"Nothing, at first. But as a lawyer and a Christian I knew that killing someone, besides being a crime, was a sin. I could go to hell for it. Then I repented and confessed. I was repentant and was absolved. I'm going to heaven, understand? My repentance was genuine. Divine justice has subtleties that man's justice lacks. But that's not the pardon that anguishes me."

"Want me to take you to the library?"

"No. Actually, I suspect that Macauley is an idiot. The others, even though they wrote some interesting things about my ancestors, are idiots too. Everything tires me. I no longer find Lou's nudity pleasurable. Heraclitus said that nothing is permanent except change. But I don't want to go to heaven."

"That's none of my business."

"Yes, it is."

"I don't want to hear your proposal."

"There's a lot of money in that cigar box."

"I'm not interested."

"Please. I don't want to go to heaven."

Suddenly he's crying. His voice is thin and pleading, like a child's. "Please, help me, I don't want to go to heaven."

I wait for him to stop crying.

"All right," I say. "As far as I'm concerned, you can go to hell."

He explains how I can help him. A glass of water and two boxes of Lexotan. Each box has twenty small, pink pills. Generic name bromazepan.

I place a glass, a bottle of water, and two boxes of pills on the night table. He's lying down, his legs crossed.

"From the start I knew I could count on you. Raise me up so I can lean against the pillows."

"Are you really sure you don't want to go to heaven?"

"You understand me."

The Lexotan pills are small, and he swallows them two at a time, sitting up with his back supported by the pillows.

"I once wanted to live a long time, to watch all my enemies die. But as soon as one enemy dies you remember another. Or you invent another. They never end."

He takes the forty pills with several glasses of water. The bottle is empty.

He stretches out in the bed again, his legs crossed.

"I have to die alone."

I get the cigar box with the money. I go to my room.

Much later the bell rings and I go to the old man's room, but he didn't ring the bell. He's lying motionless on the bed, his legs crossed. His serene face doesn't suggest that he went to purgatory, or worse.

The bell is from the front door. Lou.

"I came to finish our conversation. May I come in?"

I step aside. She comes in.

"Mr. Baglioni?"

"He's sleeping."

"Are you surprised I came today? At this hour?"

"Not very. You have your nurse's uniform on."

She goes to her room. I hear a car alarm in the street. I take the living room telephone off the hook.

Lou's white uniform doesn't have a wrinkle. She comes toward me. Her light-brown eyes have a green mark around the iris. I delicately open the button of Lou's white blouse and caress one of her breasts. Lou closes her eyes. I re-button the blouse. Lou looks at me as if she knows who I am, as if there were no barriers between us and she could confide in me now.

She takes my hand. We go to her room. I smell her perfume. She removes her uniform. I get naked before she does; I have fewer clothes to take off.

In bed, she says incomprehensible things, mixed with screams and sighs. She strains to give herself; she wants to come.

Afterward she sleeps with one arm on my chest. She wakes up for a moment and asks, "Am I better than the plastic doll?" and I answer yes.

I spend the rest of the night awake, thinking. She wakes up a little before morning. She stretches.

"Do you want more?" Lou asks shyly, knowing that to be more seductive. I don't feel like it, but I say yes. She's calmer now and satisfies herself, without screams, without sighs.

Lou goes to take a bath. I remain in bed, thinking. She returns naked from the bathroom.

"Do you want me to put on the uniform?"

"No. You can wear the other clothes."

Lou has a pretty body, when she moves without concerning herself with my presence.

"The old man told me he no longer enjoys your nudity."

"He said that?"

"Were you nude in front of him?"

She is slow to reply. "I would take off my clothes, and he'd ask me to walk around the room. But he never touched me. It was a quick thing. He would go to sleep right away. Once he cried. No, he cried twice, thinking about the life he'd led. Are you angry?"

"No. And when he'd go to sleep you'd lie down on the sofa and sleep naked too."

"How did you know? Did Mr. Baglioni tell you?"

"Your unwrinkled uniform. And the smell of perfume on the sofa."

"I'm hungry," Lou says.

I make her coffee with cream. I put raspberry jam on the toast.

"You came down from heaven for me," Lou says, chewing the toast.

"The old man died."

"What?"

"Mr. Baglioni died."

"My God. Why didn't you tell me? Him dead and us, us doing that."

"He killed himself. He took forty pills."

Lou gets up and runs to the bedroom. She leans over the old man. He's dead and cold.

"Poor thing," Lou says.

"He asked to be by himself."

I take Lou to my room. I get the cigar box full of hundred-dollar bills.

"He told me to give you this." After all, she paraded nude in front of him, gave him his final moments of joy.

"You killed Mr. Baglioni," she says with a deep sigh.

"Go on, take it."

"I don't want that money."

"You have to accept it. It was his last request."

I get my suitcase and put my things in it. Lou watches me, confused.

"Call the doctor, the one whose name is in the instructions, and tell him that through my negligence the old man got hold of the pills. I called you and like a coward left you to face the music. Don't worry. The doctor will write out a death certificate; the lawyer will take care of the funeral. The lawyer's name is also in the instructions. Nobody's going to be upset at his death."

"I am."

"Nobody else. Don't worry. Excuse me for leaving this for you to do. I have my reasons."

"Will we see each other again?"

"I don't know."

"Give me your phone number."

"I don't have a telephone."

She writes her addresses and phone numbers, at home and at the hospital, on a piece of paper. She grabs me, kisses me. I have a hard time pulling away from her grasp.

"I'm going to take this book." I pick up the book of panegyrics.

"Don't desert me," Lou says at the door.

In the street, after destroying the cover and tearing out most of the book's pages, I throw everything in the trash. My homage to the old man.

I go to the Hotel Itajubá, downtown.

I take off my shoes, lie down, and wait for night to come.

TRIALS OF A YOUNG WRITER

THE DAY GOT OFF to a bad start when I went to the beach in the morning. I never could look at the sea; it makes me sick. So I'd cross Avenida Atlântica with my eyes closed, then turn around, open my eyes, and walk backwards through the sand till I found my place, where I would sit with my back to the ocean. Crossing the street I felt a sudden fear, as if a car were about to hit me, and opened my eyes. I didn't see any cars, but I did see the ocean, just for a second, but a single instant of that Dantesque vision, that horrendous blue-green mass, was enough to make me break into a cold sweat and start vomiting, right there on the sidewalk. When the attack was over, I went home, took off my trunks, and collapsed onto the bed, exhausted, but then the doorbell rang, and when I looked through the peephole I saw a hooded figure in the darkened hallway. I was terrified. I was all by myself–Lygia was away. It could only be a thief, or a murderer; things weren't going well in the city. I tried to call the police, but the phone wasn't working, and the cloaked figure was ringing the bell insistently, tattering my nerves. "Help!" I screamed out the window, my voice weak from fear, but the street noise prevented anyone from hearing me, or else they couldn't be bothered. The bell was still ringing, the masked man wasn't about to leave, and I was naked, in the apartment, livid with fear and not knowing what to do. Then I remembered there was a large knife in the kitchen. I opened the door, brandishing the knife menacingly, but it was an elderly nun, standing there in that black thing they wear on their heads. I had made a mistake. When she saw me naked, holding the knife, the nun ran screaming down the hallway. I closed the door, relieved, and went back to bed, but a little later the bell rang again; it was the police. I opened the door and the policeman handed me a summons to testify on Monday, based on the nun's complaint that, according to her, she had knocked on my door to ask for alms for orphans and had been threatened with death. "Aren't you ashamed to walk around naked?" the policeman asked. Unbelievable. You couldn't even go naked in your own home. Sunday was even more complicated. Lygia, who had returned unexpectedly, saw me at the movies with another girl, and right there in the middle of the film started hammering on me. Talk about a scandal. I needed twenty stitches in my head. "I can't go on living with you. Look what you did to me," I said when she came to pick me up at the hospital. Lygia opened her purse, showed me an enormous black revolver, and said, "If you cheat on me with another woman, I'll kill you." All this confusion began much earlier, when I won the Academy's poetry prize and my picture was in the paper; I thought I'd achieve instant fame, with women falling into my arms. Time went by and nothing of the sort happened. One day I went to the ophthalmologist, and when I told the receptionist, "Profession: Writer," she asked, "Driver?" My fame had lasted twenty-four hours. That was when Lygia showed up. She came into my apartment, agitated and yearning, saying, "You don't know what I had to overcome to find out where you lived. O my idol, do with me what you will." I was moved. The world gave no heed to my accomplishments and this girl comes from afar to prostrate herself at my feet. Before we went to bed she said, dramatically, "I kept the treasure of my purity and youth for you and I'm happy." Anyway, she had nowhere to go, so she installed herself in my apartment, cooked for me and did some sewing work for others (despite being a bad seamstress), kept the place in order, typed the long novel I was writing, and did the grocery shopping with her own money. It was a nice arrangement, the only bad part being that she forced me to work eight hours a day on the novel—"Just talk," she'd say, while she typed at a fast clip. She also kept an eye on my drinking, and when I told her all writers drank, she said that wasn't true. Machado de Assis didn't drink, and it was thanks to her I hadn't turned into a poor and wretched alcoholic. I could take all that, but when she bashed me, I decided it was time to find a way out before she put a bullet in me. One good method was to feign impotence, something no man does, not even to save his own skin, but I was desperate enough to run the risk of bumping into Lygia on the street and having her point her large, bony finger at me and tell people, "There he is, winner of the Academy prize and he can't get it up!" When I told Lygia the situation, she dragged me to the doctor and said, "Doctor, don't you think he's awfully young to be impotent? It must be a virus, or worms. I want you to make him take all the tests." The doctor looked at me and said, "Didn't you win a prize from the Academy?" That's life. We returned home and went to bed. As soon as Lygia was asleep, I got up and took the revolver from her purse, planning to throw it in the trash. But the building where we lived was old and had no garbage chute, so I stood there with the revolver in my hand, and all I could think of was Marcel Proust with his tiny mustache and a flower in his lapel, brandishing his umbrella at the heavens and exclaiming *"Zut! Zut! Zut!"* I finally decided to go out and throw the weapon into the sewer. It was late at night, and as I was bending over the gutter, trying to push the gun through the grate, a black guy with a knife in his hand came up to me and said, "Hand over the dough and your watch or I'll stick you." *Merde*, my Japanese quartz watch, which I don't take off even when I sleep, that's accurate to within two seconds a year! I got up, and that was when the black guy saw the revolver in my hand. He stepped back in fright, but it was too late; I had already pulled the trigger. Bang! The black guy fell to the ground. I ran home saying, "I killed a black guy, I killed a black guy!" while in my multilayered thought Joyce was asking his sister if a priest could be buried in his cassock, if municipal elections could be held in

Dublin in the month of October, until I got to the room, still holding the revolver—*zut! zut! zut!*—and, without realizing what I was doing, put it back in Lygia's purse. I spent a sleepless night. When Lygia woke up I said, "You can kill me, but I'm leaving," and started getting dressed. Lygia threw herself at my feet and said, "Don't abandon me, especially now that you're in fashion with your slick black hair. You'll be used by other women, we were made for each other, without me you'll never finish your novel, if you leave me I'll kill myself and leave a terrible farewell note." I took a close look at her and saw that Lygia was speaking the absolute truth; for an instant I was of two minds. Which was better for a young writer: a prize from the Academy, or a woman killing herself over him and leaving a farewell note that blames him for her desperate gesture of love? "As far as I'm concerned, the novel is finished," I said derisively, slamming the door as I left. I stood in the hall for some time, expecting Lygia to open the door and call after me, as she always did when we fought, but that day nothing happened. I was feeling alone and wanted to go back, and, on top of everything else, I was worried about the death of the black guy, but I went ahead and walked the streets until I stopped in a bar for a beer. There was a woman at the next table, and I smiled at her. She smiled back, and soon we were at the same table. She was a student nurse, but what she really liked was film and poetry. Fernando Pessoa. Drummond, Camões (his lyrical works), the same old stuff, Fellini, Godard, Buñuel, Bergman, always the same thing, cripes, always the same people. Of course the idiot had no idea who I was. When I said I was a writer I noticed her face light up in expectation, but when I told her my name, she asked dispiritedly, "Who?" I repeated it, and she gave a sickly smile. She'd never heard of me. We drank, and there was a delightful fog in my head, with Conrad saying "I lived through all that." The girl repeated the question, "What do you write about?" "About people," I said, "My story is about people who never learned to die," and we drank some more. "Write a love story," the nurse said, and it was already late at night when I headed home, went in tripping over myself, and said to Lygia, who was asleep in bed, "Is what we're writing a love story?" But Lygia, still in a deep sleep, didn't answer. Then I saw the note on the night table, next to the bottle of sleeping pills: *José: Farewell. Without you I cannot go on living. I don't blame you for anything. I forgive you; may God grant that someday you become a good writer, however unlikely that seems. I would continue living with you, even if you are impotent, for that's not your fault either, you poor man. Lygia Castelo Branco.* I shook Lygia forcefully, but she was in a coma. I tried to make a call but the telephone wasn't working, *zut, zut,* Gustave, *le mot juste,* I ran down the stairs, and when I got to the pay phone, I saw I didn't have any change, and at that time of night everything was closed, and suddenly—damn!—a mugger appeared, of all the rotten luck, but no, no. I recognized the mugger. It was the same black guy I'd shot. He was alive! He recognized me too and ran off, perhaps from fear of being shot again. I ran after him, shouting, "Hey! You got change for the phone? My wife is sick, I have to call for help"—and we ran a thousand yards until he stopped, breathing with difficulty; he was undernourished and sickly and, panting, barely managed to say, "Please don't shoot me. I'm married and have kids to support." I said, "I want change for the telephone." He had one coin to lend me; it was tied to a nylon string. I called the emergency ambulance service, retrieved the coin, and returned it to the thief, asking if he wouldn't like to come to my place, for moral support. We went, and the thief, whose name was Enéas, made coffee for us while I poured out my troubles. "Don't take it the wrong way," Enéas said, "but I think your wife's kicked the bucket. She's cold as a lizard." The ambulance arrived, and the doctor examined Lygia. He said, "I'll have to notify the police. Don't touch anything. All suicide cases have to be reported." He looked at me strangely—had he read the note? When he heard the police mentioned, Enéas said it was time for him to go—you know how it is, sorry about that, buddy—and he left, leaving me alone with the body. I cried a bit—to tell the truth, just a little bit, not from lack of feeling but because my thoughts were on other things. I sat down at the typewriter. *José, my great love: farewell. I cannot force you to love me with the same fervor that I dedicate to you. I'm jealous of all the beautiful women who hover around trying to seduce you; I'm jealous of the hours you spend writing your major novel. Oh yes, love of my life, I know a writer needs solitude to create, but my petty soul, the soul of a woman in love, cannot bear to share you with any other person or thing. My dear lover, our moments together were wonderful! I deeply regret not being able to finish the book that will surely be a masterpiece. Farewell, farewell! Love me always, remember me, forgive me. Place a rose by my grave each year. Your Lygia Castelo Branco.* I signed the letter with Lygia's rounded handwriting and put it on the night stand, then took the letter she had written, tore it to tiny pieces, burned the pieces, and flushed the ashes down the toilet. Impotent and a bad writer—*merde!* What did I do for her to treat me like that? I was thoughtful and impassioned, wasn't I? While thinking these thoughts I went to the refrigerator for a beer. I treated Lygia with consideration and dignity, didn't I? If anybody lorded it over anybody, it was her over me. She was her own boss; I was the one who had to exercise, diet, stop drinking—I got up for another beer—and now she said it was unlikely I'd become a great writer. What had I done? I'd loved her and this is how she repaid me, by swallowing a bottle of sleeping pills and leaving behind a slanderous letter? I got another beer and looked at Lygia in the bed, her face now in repose. She was pretty, even more so pale like that, without makeup, her freckles showing, without lipstick—I got up and drank another beer—poor Lygia, why did you get involved with a writer? I went over to her and took her by the shoulder, which was starting to get stiff, as well as cold, and said, "Well? Well? Why'd you get mixed up with a writer? We're all disgusting egotists who treat women as if they were our slaves. You were the one who made what little money we had to support ourselves with, and I created philosophy, right? Why?" And I stood up, got another beer, returned to Lygia's side, since I hadn't finished my speech, and went on: "We threw away our life, believing that two people could become one, poor hopeful innocents that we were." And I swear that at that very moment Lygia's chest swelled, as if she had taken a breath. "The worms are going to eat you, my love"—and I had another beer, *zut*, why was there so much beer, she was really a great housekeeper—"the worms are going to eat you, but I want you to know one truth"—and at that moment my drunken memory failed me and I stood there beside the cold corpse not knowing what to say. I kissed Lygia's lips with an unbearable feeling of disgust, then went to the refrigerator for the last bottle of beer—she wasn't that great a housekeeper after all, since I was still thirsty—and that was when the police arrived. Two men. One asked me right away who I was and the other picked up the note; both of them read it, and after that they ignored me, resuming their earlier conversation, till one of them asked, "Had she seemed nervous?" They asked questions I didn't understand, time stood still, I wanted to sleep, and one of them asked, "The phone's not working? We have to call the coroner." The other said, "Killing herself over a shrimp like that. Women are crazy," and left to call the coroner from the squad car, while his partner smoked calmly—it was an oppressive morning—and from the window I could see the chimneys of all the apartment buildings spewing white smoke into the atmosphere, like an avenging angel bringing back discarded garbage, through the air. My body was slight but it was mine, like my multilayered thought. Then the forensic team arrived with their cameras, notebooks, and tape measures. And two more men showed up, in a kind of uniform that looked like a poor man's version of fancy summer wear, and tossed Lygia's body into an aluminum box and took her off to the worms—you never learned to die, unfortunate woman, not even you?—and the officer in charge told me to show up the next day to make a statement. After the autopsy, the body would be mine to dispose of—for what?—and they left, taking Lygia's note. I imagined the papers the next day: "Beautiful Woman Kills Self Over Young Writer." I'm not to blame for what happened, said the Young and Renowned Writer when interviewed by this newspaper. I deeply regret the death of this poor and disturbed creature, that's all I have to say . . . This reporter has discovered that this is not the first time a woman has killed herself over the Young Writer. Two years ago, in Minas Gerais—no, better make that Rio de Janeiro—two years ago, in Rio de Janeiro, a Frenchwoman studying anthropology . . . Enough multilayered thought, I told myself, and went out to a bar. I was on my third drink when two girls sat down at the next table and one said hi. Hi from me, and I took my glass and changed tables; one was a model who did television commercials and the other didn't do anything. "What do you do?" "I kill women." I could have said I'm a writer, but that's worse than being a killer; writers are wonderful lovers for a few months and lousy husbands for a lifetime. "How do you kill them?" "Poison, the slow poison of indifference." One of them, the one who didn't do anything, was named Iris, and the other Suzanne—call me Suzie. I don't remember anything beyond that; I got drunk and woke up the next morning with a hangover—not even thirty and already suffering memory loss like an alcoholic, not to mention seeing my palimpsest double after the fourth round. I went out and bought a few newspapers. Only one carried the story of Lygia's death: "Seamstress Kills Self In Copacabana" was the headline, on page six, and, in small print, it told how the seamstress's companion had said the woman suffered from nerves. I went to the police station and waited two hours to make a statement. The clerk fed a piece of paper into the typewriter: The Deponent stated that he co-habited as man and wife with Lygia Castelo Branco, the suicide. That on July 14th he went out for a drink, leaving Lygia in the apartment where they lived, at 435 Barata Ribeiro St., Apartment 12. That upon his return, some hours later, he found said Lygia in a coma and called an ambulance. That upon his arrival the doctor confirmed Lygia's death. That Lygia left a note clarifying that she had committed suicide. That the police, called by the doctor, arrived soon thereafter, and that the site was examined for evidence and the body removed to the Morgue. I signed where they told me to. There was a newspaper photographer at the station who asked if I had a picture of the girl—suicide, wasn't it? "A case of love run wild," I said, "and the papers didn't even take notice. Her note is touching." The photographer told me the cub reporter with him was an imbecile, a beginner who could barely write his name, and that he'd do the story himself. "What was her name again, and yours?" And he shot me from several angles while I said, "I'm a writer; I won a prize from the Academy and I'm writing a definitive novel. The nation's literature is in crisis, a pile of crap. Where are the great themes of love and death?" I went to sleep waiting for the following day, and it was all there in the paper, in a prominent spot, my picture—slim, romantic, pensive, and mysterious. Underneath, the caption read quote Death and love not found in books unquote. The headline read, "Society Designer Kills Self for Love of Celebrated Writer." "Lygia Castelo Branco, the beautiful and well-known fashion designer, killed herself yesterday after breaking off with her lover, a renowned novelist." My heart fluttered with satisfaction; the note was published in its entirety and quote Beautiful young woman kills herself but the world doesn't care unquote was written beneath Lygia's picture. The story even mentioned my book, my statement at the station, and had invented an elegant life for Lygia. The journalist was a liar, fortunately. Now down to work, I roared in my multilayered thought, and ran home, sat down at the typewriter, ready to finish my novel at one sitting, even without Anna Grigorievna Castelo Branco Snitkina. But not a single word came, not one; I looked at the blank paper, wrung my hands, bit my lips, huffed and sighed, but nothing came out. Then I tried to recall the technique I used: Lygia would type while I paced the room and dictated the words. I got up and attempted to duplicate the process, but it was impossible. I would shout a sentence, run to the typewriter, type frantically, then get up, pace, dictate another sentence, sit down, write, get up, dictate, sit down, pace, sit, get up—but I quickly saw that the words I was putting on paper were completely idiotic. With Lygia I hadn't read the words as they were being written—that's it, I thought. With Lygia I had paced around the room, throwing words at her as she speedily worked the keyboard, and I would only see the results later, sometimes the following day. I tried writing without reading what I was writing, allowing my thoughts to run free, but I saw it was one big piece of crap. And then, then, horrified, I understood everything—with trembling hand and a chill in my heart I took out the sheets that Lygia had typed and read what was written there, and the truth revealed itself brutally and irrevocably. It was Lygia who was writing my novel—the seamstress, the slave of the great hack writer. Not a single word there was really mine; she had written everything, and it was truly going to be a great novel and I, the young alcoholic, hadn't even realized what was happening. I lay down on the bed, wanting to die. Yes, yes, as that Russian said, life had taught me to think, but thinking hadn't taught me to live, and then the doorbell rang and a bald man came in, dressed to the nines, red kerchief in his pocket, ruby ring, gilded tie with a pearl tiepin, colored shirt, and striped suit. He introduced himself as Detective Jacob and asked me to write Lygia's name in full on a piece of paper, which I did, and he left and I lay back down on the bed, sad and hungry, so hungry that I got up and went to the bar, where I had several bottles of beer, which deadened the pain. I went home again and re-read Lygia's novel: a masterpiece with no need of revision, it could be published just as it was, and only someone who knew it was unfinished—and nobody knew that—could be aware that something was missing. But now that I thought about it, just what was missing? What was Lygia waiting for? That was easy. Lygia was never going to finish; the novel she pretended to be writing was what linked me to her. Lygia was afraid that the end of the book would also be the end of our involvement, and in my multilayered thought there came the certainty that Lygia hadn't meant to commit suicide, only to frighten me. If she had wanted to kill herself, she could have put a bullet in her head; she handled firearms perfectly, so why take those damned pills? The bell rang, and it was Jacob, the detective, wearing a different set of colorful clothes, a different tiepin. He came in and sat down, saying, "My feet are killing me. Mind if I take off my shoes?" He was wearing brightly colored socks and his feet reeked of perfume, a stench that got worse when he took a small vial from his pocket and sprinkled more perfume over his socks. "You're in a pickle, my boy. The lab proved that you forged the dead woman's signature and the pills were bought with a prescription in your name, besides which you tried to kill a nun for no reason other than to satisfy your now proven violent nature." I protested, "Violent? I'm a considerate and gentle soul. You just don't know me—" And I stopped, for Jacob brought his right foot up to his nose, sniffed, and said, "Nothing I hate worse than smelly feet. And besides," he continued, "there's the matter of the fight between you and the deceased, plus the doctor's statement, and last but not least"— Jacob took from his pocket a tortoise shell shoehorn with a hotel's name on it and carefully worked his feet into his shoes—"Last but not least, two girls showed up at the precinct who said they heard you say in a bar that you had poisoned some women. Let's go, my boy." "I can explain everything—" I said, but Jacob cut me off. "Explain it downtown, let's go." I took the book and we went downstairs together, I got in the police car, my multilayered thought, famous novelist accused of murder, publishers lining up outside his cell, accla—

THE OTHER

I would arrive at my office at eight-thirty in the morning. The car would stop at the door of the building and I would get out, walk ten or fifteen steps, and go in.

Like all executives, I spent my mornings making phone calls, reading memos, dictating letters to my secretary, and getting worked up over problems. By lunchtime, I'd already put in a day's work. But I always had the impression that I hadn't done anything useful.

I'd have lunch in a hour, sometimes an hour and a half, in one of the nearby restaurants, and return to the office. There were days when I spoke on the phone dozens of times. There were so many letters that my secretary, or one of the assistants, would sign for me. And always, at the end of the day, I had the impression of not having done everything I needed to do. I was in a race against time. When there was a holiday in the middle of the week I would get irritated, because it meant less time for me. I took work home every day; at home I could be more productive, because I wasn't being called on phone so often.

One day, my heart started racing. The same day, in fact, when, as I was arriving at the office in the morning, a guy appeared next to me, on the sidewalk, a guy who went with me to the door, saying, "Sir, sir, can you help me?" I gave him some change and went inside. It was shortly after this, as I was talking on the phone to São Paulo, that my heart started acting up. It beat fiercely for several minutes, leaving me exhausted. I had to lie down on the sofa until it passed. I was dizzy, sweating profusely, and I almost fainted.

That afternoon I went to the cardiologist. He examined me in minute detail, even ordering a stress electrocardiogram, and finally told me I needed to lose weight and change my lifestyle. I thought that was funny. Then he recommended I stop working for a time, but I said that was impossible. Finally he prescribed a diet and told me to walk at least twice a day.

The next day, at lunchtime, as I was leaving for the walk prescribed by the doctor, the same guy stopped me to ask for money. He was a white man, husky, with long brown hair. I gave him some money and continued on my way.

The doctor had said candidly that if I didn't take care I could have a heart attack at any moment. I took two tranquilizers that day, but they weren't enough to completely relieve the tension. That night I didn't take any work home. But time wouldn't pass. I tried reading a book, but my attention was elsewhere, at the office. I turned the television on, but I couldn't stand more than ten minutes. I came back from my after dinner walk and became impatient, irritated, and sat in the armchair, reading the newspaper.

At lunchtime the same guy sidled up to me, asking for money. "Every day?" I asked. "Sir," he replied, "my mother is dying. She needs medicine. I don't know anybody good in the whole world, only you." I gave him twenty reais.

For a few days the guy disappeared. One day, I was walking at lunchtime when he suddenly appeared beside me. "Sir, my mother died." Without stopping, and accelerating my pace, I answered, "I'm very sorry." He lengthened his stride, keeping up with me, and said, "She died." I tried to get away from him and began walking quickly, almost running. But he ran after me, saying, "Died, died, died," extending both arms in a labored gesture, as if he expected his mother's coffin to be placed in his hands. Finally, I stopped and asked, panting, "How much?"

For five hundred he could bury his mother. I don't know why, but I took my checkbook from my pocket and wrote a check for the amount right there in the street. My hands were trembling. "Enough!" I said.

The next day I didn't go out for my walk; I had lunch at the office. It was a terrible day. Everything went wrong: papers weren't found in the files, we lost a bid over a few small differences, and a financial planning error required a long series of complex budget recalculations that had to be done on an emergency footing. That night, even with the tranquilizers, I had a hard time getting to sleep.

In the morning, I left for the office and, to a certain extent, things got a little better. At noon I went out for my walk.

I saw that the guy who asked me for money was standing on the corner, half hidden, spying on me, waiting for me to pass. I turned around and headed in the opposite direction. Soon I heard the sound of heels on the sidewalk, as if someone were running after me. I walked faster, feeling a twinge in my heart; it was as if I were being pursued by someone, a childish feeling of fear that I tried to fight, but at that instant he overtook me, saying, "Sir, sir." Without stopping, I asked, "What is it now?" Staying at my side, he said, "Sir, you have to help me; I don't have anyone in the world." I replied with as much authority as I could put into my voice, "Get a job." He said, "I don't know how to do anything; you have to help me." We ran down the street. I had the impression that people were looking at us strangely. "I don't have to help you at all," I replied. "Yes, you do, otherwise you don't know what might happen," and he held me by the arm and looked at me, and for the first time I really saw his face, cynical and vengeful. My heart was pounding from nervousness and exhaustion. "It's the last time," I said, stopping and giving him some money, I don't know how much.

But it wasn't the last time. Every day he would show up, imploring and menacing, walking beside me, ruining my health, saying it's the last time, sir, but it never was. My blood pressure was rising and my heart was on the point of exploding just thinking about him. I didn't want to see the guy anymore. Was it my fault he was poor?

I decided to stop working for a time. I spoke with my partners, who agreed to my being away for two months.

The first week was hard. It's not easy to suddenly stop working. I felt lost, not knowing what to do. But little by little I got used to it. My appetite improved. I started sleeping better and smoking less. I watched television, read, took a nap after lunch, walked twice as much as I did before, and felt great. I was turning into a calm man and was thinking seriously about changing my way of life, not working so hard.

One day I was going out for my usual walk when he, the supplicant, showed up unexpectedly. Hell, how had he discovered my address? "Sir, don't abandon me!" His voice was full of pain and resentment. "You're all I have in the world, don't do this to me again. I need a little bit of money, this is the last time, I swear it!" And he leaned his body very close to mine as we walked, and I could smell the sour, rotten breath of a hungry man. He was taller than me, strong and threatening.

I went toward my house, with him accompanying me, his face staring into mine, watching me curiously, suspiciously, implacably, until we arrived. I said, "Wait here."

I closed the door and went to my room. I returned, opened the door, and, when he saw me, he said, "Don't do it, sir, you're all I have in the world." He didn't finish speaking, or if he did, I didn't hear him because of the sound of the shot. He fell to the ground, and I saw he was a skinny boy, with pimples on his face, and a paleness that even the blood that covered his cheeks could not hide.

HAPPY NEW YEAR

I SAW ON TELEVISION that the chic stores were selling fancy clothes like crazy for society women to wear on New Year's Eve. I also saw that the shops that sell expensive food and booze were sold out.

"Mange, I'm going to have to wait till daybreak to get some rum, a dead chicken, and manioc flour from the voodoo people."

Mange went into the bathroom and said, "What a stench."

"Go somewhere else to piss, there's no water."

Mange left and went to piss on the stairway.

"Where'd you boost the TV?" Mange asked.

"I didn't boost shit. I bought it. The receipt's on top of it. Mange, you think I'm dumb enough to keep anything hot in my hideout?"

"I'm starving," Mange said.

"In the morning we'll pig out on the voodoo offerings," I said, just to rattle his cage.

"Don't count on me," said Mange. "You remember Crispim? He kicked over an offering here on Borges de Medeiros and his leg turned all black. They had to cut it off at the hospital and now there he is, fucked up and using a crutch."

Mange always was superstitious. Not me. I went to high school, I know how to read, write, and take square roots. I'll kick over any offering I want to.

We lit some joints and watched the soap. A piece of shit. We changed channels to a Western. More crap.

"All the society women are wearing their new clothes, they're going to start the new year by dancing with their arms in the air. You ever see how those white broads dance? They raise their arms in the air, I think it's to show their armpits, what they really want is to show their pussies, but they don't have the balls for it and they show their armpits instead. They all cheat on their husbands. Did you know that all they do is spread their cunts around?"

"Too bad they ain't spreading it our way," said Mange. He was speaking slowly, mockingly, tired, sick.

"Mange, you got no teeth, you're cross-eyed, poor, and black. You think high-society women're gonna put out for you? Look, Mange, all you can do is jerk off. Close your eyes and go to it."

"I'd like to be rich, leave this shit behind! So many rich people and me fucked over."

Zequinha came into the room, saw Mange beating off, and said, "What's goin' on, Mange?"

"I lost it, I lost it, it's impossible like this," said Mange.

"Why didn't you go in the bathroom to beat your meat?" said Zequinha.

"The bathroom stinks to high heaven," said Mange.

"I don't have any water."

"The women in the project aren't putting out anymore?" asked Zequinha.

"He was paying homage to a cool blonde in an evening gown, dripping with jewels."

"She was naked," said Mange.

"I can see things are going piss-poor for you guys," said Zequinha.

"He wants to eat the voodoo offerings," said Mange.

"I was kidding," I said. After all, Zequinha and I had held up a supermarket in Leblon. It wasn't a lot of dough, but we'd spent a long time in the red-light district in São Paulo, drinking and screwing women. We respected each other.

"To tell the truth, things ain't going too good for me neither," said Zequinha. "It's tough. The heat's not messing around, you see what they did to Bom Crioulo? Sixteen bullets in the noodle. They caught Vevé and strangled him. And Maggot, shit! Maggot! We grew up together in Caxias, the guy was so nearsighted he couldn't see from here to there, and he stuttered–they caught him and threw him in the Guandu, broke every bone in his body."

"It was even worse with Tripod. They set him on fire. Burnt to a crisp. The Men ain't playin' softball," said Mange. "And I ain't eatin' no voodoo chicken."

"Day after tomorrow you're gonna see."

"See what?" Zequinha asked.

"I'm just waiting for Lambretta to get in from São Paulo."

"Shit, you doing business with Lambretta?" said Zequinha.

"All his tools are here."

"Here?" said Zequinha. "You're crazy!"

I laughed.

"What kind of pieces you got?" asked Zequinha.

"A Thompson submachine gun, a sawed-off 12 carbine, and two Magnums."

"Motherfucker," said Zequinha. "You got all that and you're sitting around jerking off?"

"Waitin' for daybreak to eat voodoo offerings," said Mange. He'd be a hit on TV talking like that–people would die laughing.

We smoked. We emptied a bottle of booze.

"Can I see the goods?" Zequinha said.

We went down the stairs–the elevator wasn't working–to Dona Candinha's apartment. We knocked. The old lady opened the door.

"Good evening, Dona Candinha, I came to get the package."

"Is Lambretta here?" the old black woman asked.

"Yes," I said, "he's upstairs."

The old woman brought the package. She moved with difficulty; the weight was too much for her. "Be careful, boys," she said.

We climbed the stairs and returned to my apartment. I opened the package. First I loaded the Thompson and gave it to Zequinha to hold. "I love this machine, tatatatatata!" Zequinha said.

"It's old but it never lets you down," I said.

Zequinha picked up the Magnum. "Beautiful, beautiful," he said. Then he picked up the 12, put the butt against his shoulder and said, "I'm gonna put a bullet from this beauty in the chest of some cop, up close, you know what I mean, to throw the fucker up against the wall and leave him stuck there."

We put everything on the table and stood there looking at it. We smoked a little more.

"When are you gonna use the material?" said Zequinha.

"On the second. We're hitting a bank in Penha. Lambretta wants to score the first goal of the year."

"He's a vain kind of guy," said Zequinha.

"He's got good reason to be. He's worked in São Paulo, Curitiba, Florianópolis, Porto Alegre, Vitória, Niterói, not to mention here in Rio. Over thirty banks."

"Yeah, but they say he takes it in the ass," said Zequinha.

"I don't know if he does or not, and I don't have the guts to ask. He's never come on to me."

"You ever seen him with a woman?" said Zequinha.

"No, never did. Beats me, it could be true, but what does it matter?"

"A man shouldn't spread his cheeks. Much less an important guy like Lambretta," said Zequinha.

"Important guys do whatever they feel like," I said.

"That's true," said Zequinha.

We stopped talking and smoked.

"The irons in our hands and we do nothing," said Zequinha.

"The goods are Lambretta's. And just where would we use them at this time of night?"

Zequinha sucked in the air, pretending he had something caught in his teeth. I think he was hungry too.

"I was thinking we could bust into one of them fancy houses where they're having a party. The women are wearing all kinds of jewelry and I got a guy who'll buy everything I take to him. And the dudes have wads of dough in their wallets. Would you believe there's a ring worth five grand and a necklace worth fifteen at that fence I know? He pays cash up-front."

The grass gave out. The booze too. It started to rain.

"There goes your voodoo food," said Mange.

"What house? You got one in mind?"

"No, but rich people have houses all over the place. We'll boost a car and go hunting."

I put the Thompson in a shopping bag along with the ammo. I gave one Magnum to Mange, the other to Zequinha. I stuck the carbine in my belt, barrel down, and put on a coat. I got three women's stockings and a pair of scissors. "Let's go," I said.

We boosted an Opala. We headed toward São Conrado. We passed several houses that weren't right, either they were too close to the street or there were too many people, until we found the perfect spot. There was a large garden in front and the house was in the rear, isolated. The people were listening to Carnival music, but only a few were singing. We pulled the stockings over our heads. I used the scissors to cut eyeholes. We went in through the front door.

They were drinking and dancing in a large room when they saw us.

"This is a holdup," I shouted loudly, to drown out the sound of the record player. "Keep quiet and nobody'll get hurt. You there, turn off that goddamn record player!"

Mange and Zequinha went to look for the help and returned with three waiters and two cooks. "Everybody lay down," I said.

I counted. Twenty-five people. All of them laying down in silence, quiet like they weren't being seen or seeing anything.

"Anybody else in the house?" I asked.

"My mother. She's upstairs in her room. She's a sick old lady," said a dolled-up woman in a long red dress. She must be the owner of the house.

"Children?"

"They're in Cabo Frio with their aunt and uncle."

"Gonçalves, go up there with the plump lady and bring her mother down."

"Gonçalves?" said Mange.

"That's you. Don't you even know your name anymore, you moron?"

Mange took the woman and went upstairs.

"Inocêncio, tie the dudes up."

Zequinha tied the men up with belts, curtain cords, telephone wires, anything he could find.

We searched the guys. Very little dough. The fuckers were full of credit cards and checkbooks. The watches were good, gold and platinum. I yanked the jewels off the women. A lot of gold and diamonds. We tossed it all into the bag.

Mange came down the stairs by himself.

"Where're the women?" I said.

"They mouthed off and I had to learn them some respect."

I went upstairs. The plump woman was on the bed, her clothes torn, her tongue hanging out. Dead as a doornail. Why'd she play games instead of putting out right off the bat? Mange was horny. Fucked and underpaid. I cleaned out the jewels. The old woman was in the hallway, on the floor. She'd bought it too. Her hair was all done up, her beehive hairdo dyed blond, her face wrinkled. She was waiting for the new year in a new outfit, but she was already on the other side. I think she died of fright. I yanked off the necklaces, brooches, and rings. One ring didn't want to come off. Feeling disgust, I wet the old woman's finger with some saliva, but even then the ring wouldn't come off. I got pissed and bit off her finger. I stuck everything in the pillowcase. The walls of the plump woman's room were covered in leather. The bathtub was a large square of white marble that was sunk into the floor. One entire wall of mirrors. Everything perfumed. I went back to the bedroom, pushed the plump woman onto the floor, and carefully arranged the satin bedspread, so it was smooth and shiny. I took off my pants and shit on the bedspread. It was a relief, real cool. Then I wiped my ass on the bedspread, put on my pants, and went downstairs.

"Let's eat," I said, dropping the pillowcase into the bag. The men and women on the floor were quiet and scared shitless, like little sheep. To scare them even more, I said, "Any fucker who moves I'll blow his brains out."

Then, suddenly, one of them said calmly, "Don't get excited, take whatever you want, we won't do anything."

I looked at him. He was wearing a colored silk ascot around his neck.

"And you can eat and drink as much as you like," he said.

Son of a bitch. The drinks, the food, the jewels, the money, all that was just crumbs to them. They had lots more in the bank. To them we were nothing more than three flies in the sugar bowl.

"What's your name?"

"Mauricio," he said.

"Mr. Mauricio, would you please be so good as to stand up?"

He got up. I untied his arms.

"Thank you very much," he said. "It's obvious you're a well-mannered and educated man. You can all leave now, we won't report it to the police." While he said this he was looking at the others, who were laying quiet and terrified on the floor, and made a gesture with his hands spread, as if to say, "Relax, friends, I've got this asshole eating out of my hand."

"Inocêncio, you through eating? Bring me one of those turkey drumsticks." The table had enough food to feed the entire penitentiary. I ate the drumstick. I picked up the carbine and loaded both barrels.

"Mr. Maurício, would you kindly stand in front of that wall?"

He leaned against the wall.

"No, not touching it. About six feet away from it. A little bit more this way. That's it. Thank you very much."

I shot him right in the chest, emptying both barrels—a tremendous thunderclap. The powerful impact threw the guy against the wall. He slid down slowly and ended up sitting on the floor. There was a hole in his chest that was big enough for a loaf of bread.

"See? He didn't stick to the wall for shit."

"It's gotta be wood, a door. Walls don't work," Zequinha said. The guys on the floor had their eyes shut and weren't moving a muscle. The only thing you could hear was Mange belching.

"You there, get up," Zequinha said. The bastard had chosen a thin guy with long hair.

"Please," the guy said softly.

"Back to the wall," said Zequinha.

I loaded both barrels of the 12. "You shoot, the kick hurt my shoulder. Brace the butt good or it'll break your collarbone."

"Watch how this one sticks." Zequinha shot. The guy flew, his feet lifted off the floor. It was beautiful, like he'd sprung backward. He banged against the door and stuck there. It wasn't for long, but the guy's body was pinned to the wood by the heavy lead.

"Didn't I tell you?" Zequinha rubbed his aching shoulder. "That's one motherfucker of a cannon."

"Ain't you gonna screw one of them fancy ladies?" Mange asked.

"I don't feel like it. I'm disgusted with these women. I don't give a shit about them. I only screw women I like."

"What about you . . . Inocêncio?"

"I think I'm gonna have me that little dark-skinned one."

The girl tried to get away, but Zequinha slapped her a couple of times. She calmed down, and while he did her on the sofa she kept quiet, her eyes open, looking at the ceiling.

"Let's go," I said. We filled towels and pillowcases with jewels, money, food.

"Thank you all very much for your cooperation," I said. No one replied.

We left. We got in the Opala and went home.

I told Mange, "Ditch the wheels on some deserted street in Botafogo, take a taxi, and come back." Zequinha and I got out.

"This building is really fucked up," said Zequinha, as we climbed the dirty, ramshackle stairs with the goods.

"Fucked up, but a good address, near the beach. You'd like me to go live in Nilópolis?"

We were worn out when we got upstairs. I put the tools in the package, the jewels and the money in the sack, and took it to the old lady's apartment.

"Dona Candinha," I said, pointing to the sack, "it's hot."

"Never you mind, son. The Men don't come here."

We went back upstairs. I put the bottles and the food on top of a towel on the floor. Zequinha wanted to start drinking, but I wouldn't let him. "We're gonna wait for Mange."

When Mange arrived, I filled the glasses and said, "May the new year be better. Happy New Year."

THE DWARF

IT DOESN'T MATTER how it was that an unemployed bank teller like me met a woman like Paula, but I'm going to tell anyway. She ran me over in her big car and took me to the hospital and said on the way, "It was my fault, I was talking on my cell phone and got distracted; my husband hates for me to drive." When we got to the hospital I told everybody it was my fault. She gave a sigh of relief and whispered, "Thank you." They operated on my leg, put a bunch of screws in it, and left me on a cot in the hallway, because the hospital was so full that there wasn't any room in the wards.

The next morning, she came to visit me. She asked if I'd spent the night in the corridor. That was absurd; she said she was going to take me to a private clinic. I explained that I was okay, there was no need for her to worry. I wanted her to leave right away; they'd dressed me in a gown that showed my butt if I turned in bed—I mean, on the cot. She left a box of chocolates that I gave to the girl who was taking care of me, Sabrina. I think she was an aide, but she liked to pretend she was a nurse.

A few days later the woman returned with another box of chocolates. Before she could say anything, Sabrina appeared and asked how she had gotten in there and she said she had the director's permission and that she felt responsible for me because she'd run me over, that I'd need crutches and she'd brought crutches for me. "No need," Sabrina said, "he has them already and please leave because it's time for his tests." The woman asked if I wanted her to go and I said I did and she left and Sabrina touched my leg and whenever Sabrina touched my leg I got a hard-on, now that the leg didn't ache as much. "Throw that rich bitch's box of candy in the trash, okay?"

That same afternoon Sabrina showed up and said I was one lucky guy or else a friend of the mayor's; I was being transferred to a ward. When Sabrina appeared, my heart beat fast and every day I found her more and more attractive and was getting hard when she touched me, but every night I dreamed about the woman who had run me over, her fine black hair, her body as white as a sheet of paper. And that same day Sabrina gave me a newspaper clipping with the woman's picture. "Take a look at your deadly socialite." That was when I found out her name was Paula. "Of course you didn't know her name, you idiot, she wasn't about to give you her name for fear you'd ask for compensation. What rich people like more than anything is money, so she gives you chocolates that cost next to nothing so you won't take any action against her. Tear up that photo right now."

I hid the photo and went on dreaming about Paula and getting a hard-on every time Sabrina touched my leg and looking at Paula's picture when Sabrina wasn't around. When I was released, Sabrina asked if I wanted her to take me home and I said it wasn't necessary, I'd make it on my own. She insisted, and I was harsh, "No need," and she became annoyed and I got sad. Sabrina had taken care of me, had taught me to walk on crutches, and here I was treating her like that.

Climbing the stairs to my second-floor apartment in Catumbi was very difficult, I suffered like hell. That afternoon there was a knock on the door and a woman dressed in white came in and said she was the physical therapist from the hospital and that she'd been sent to take care of me. "Sabrina sent you?" "Yes, yes," and the woman pushed my leg this way and that way and told me the exercises I had to do and that she'd be back tomorrow.

After two weeks of therapy, Sabrina showed up at my place with a present—a Tim Maia cassette. I told her that a physical therapist from the hospital came every other day to massage my leg. She didn't say anything for a time, then she said, "Physical therapist? The hospital didn't send any physical therapist. We don't even have money to buy gauze, how could we send a physical therapist for in-home service? There are lots of charlatans in that field. Let me do your therapy," and she began to move my leg and saw my hard-on and asked, "What's that?" "Grab it and see," I said, and she did. "You always got that way when I worked on your leg, think I didn't see? Don't move, I'm getting on top of you, just stay quiet," and she climbed on top of me and stuck my dick in her and we fucked and it was very good.

Sabrina returned the next day a little before the therapist arrived. When the woman showed up, Sabrina asked, "Were you sent by the hospital?" "Yes, ma'am, the hospital sent me." Sabrina bit her lip and stared at the woman doing exercises with me until she couldn't take any more and said, "You may be a physical therapist but you're not from the hospital. *I'm* from the hospital and I know all the physical therapists at the hospital. Who sent you here?" "I can't say." "Out with it, it's better for you to tell." "A charitable soul," the woman said, her eyes lowered. "Fuck that, nobody does charity for an unemployed bank teller!" Sabrina screamed, "It was that bitch who thinks money can buy anything. You tell her that Zé doesn't accept alms, do you, sweetheart?" The woman in white defended herself, "I was paid in advance, I have to deliver my service, there's still—" "It's over, over, and don't you come here anymore, isn't that right, sweetheart? Do whatever you want with the money that whore gave you, but don't come here again, go on, Zé, tell her not to come here again." I tried to calm her down, I said, "Look, Sabrina." "She can't come back here, goddamn it, if she does I'll never set foot in this place again." The therapist got her bag and left, annoyed and a bit frightened, and Sabrina climbed on top of me and we fucked.

It wasn't because Sabrina had bleached hair that I began to like her less, I mean, I liked fucking her, we bank employees are very horny, we're always getting a hard-on, it must be because we handle money all day long, or at least that's what happened with me, every woman who came to my window made me feel like fucking her, the pretty ones I mean, but they didn't have to be very pretty, sometimes I wanted to screw even the plain ones, I would get all flustered and mess up the change and get docked at the end of the month. The bank was unforgiving and I did it so often that they fired me and it was even a good thing because I felt that by not handling so much money that crazy horniness would go away and I could live in peace. But I was run over the day after they let me go and all those things started happening, Sabrina, Paula, the dwarf.

When Sabrina left, I would lie down and dream about Paula. So as not to forget what she was like, I would look at her picture all the time. My leg was getting better and I could go on top of Sabrina and could turn over in bed and could leave the house and the first thing I did was to laminate Paula's picture— the newspaper was starting to disintegrate. When Dona Alzira, the landlady who lives on the ground floor, told me my rent was paid I thought it had been Sabrina and that's when I stepped in it. We had just finished fucking and I was still on top of her when I said, "Thanks for the rent but I'm going to pay it all back. I don't like owing anything to anybody, much less the woman I'm seeing." Sabrina pushed me away hard, got out from under me, hit my leg, the one with the metal pins in it, and yelled "It was that whore, you were meeting that whore the Friday I came here and you'd disappeared, you were fucking that cow. If you see her again I'll cut your dick off while you're asleep, like that American woman did with her husband, and put it through the meat grinder. There's not a surgeon in the world who could reattach it." I swore I hadn't gone to see Pa—that woman. "You sonofabitch, you were about to say her name, you haven't forgotten her name," and Sabrina punched my leg with the metal pins several times. I tried to make a joke. "If you put my dick through the grinder, are you going to eat it like it was a hamburger?" More punches on the leg with the pins.

You can't live with a woman like that. Whenever we fucked, when we would fuck all day long and I'd put it in her two or three times—I'm not bragging, it's just the damned time I spent counting money at the bank—on those occasions, when we'd finished fucking, Sabrina would ask, "Was it like this with the others? This crazy?" And I'm no fool or anything and would say, "No, no, just with you." "You swear it's just with me?" "I swear, may my mother drop dead if I ever fucked like that with another woman." "Your mother's already dead, you sonofabitch." "I swear, may my mother come back to life if it's not true that I only fuck like that with you." That was to make us laugh, we should've laughed our heads off, it's good to laugh between screwings, but Sabrina never laughed, she only liked fucking. If she had handled as much new and old money for so long, I don't know what would have happened to her. Sabrina was persistent, "You remember the name of that bitch, don't you? Go on, admit it. One of these days I'm going to look that Paula up and put an end to this business." More vows on my part, more punches on the leg with the pins.

Sabrina went to talk with Dona Alzira. My landlady said the money had come in the mail, along with a typed sheet of paper which read, "to pay for the apartment." "Computer print," said Sabrina, "the bitch has a computer."

Sabrina wouldn't leave my place. She brought a suitcase with her things, clothes, Tim Maia records. I started getting mad at her, mad at Tim Maia, but even so we fucked fucked fucked, that damn bank, those damn crisp bills straight from the Mint. I knew what time Sabrina would arrive and before she got there I would take out Paula's picture and jerk off twice so as to go limp in bed and for her to be disappointed with me and go away. But Sabrina had ways of getting my dick up and then we'd go at it, that madness. And I was forced to take vitamins, which Sabrina shoved down my throat, and oatmeal and guaraná powder and some other foul-tasting herbal potion that she made in the kitchen.

If Sabrina knew that sometimes when I left the house the car that ran me over was parked at the corner and my heart would beat so hard that it jingled the little medals that I wear on a chain and that were given me by my mother shortly before she died, "Son, never take off these medallions of Our Lady from around your neck," and I would look at the car with its darkened windows knowing, oh I knew, that Paula was inside there with those delicate ways of hers, and the medals clinked and I couldn't take my eyes off the car clinkclinkclink and the car pulled away and I sat on the curb, feeling like crying I missed Paula so much. If Sabrina found out, my dick would end up in the meat grinder.

It had to happen sooner or later. There was a knock at the door. I opened it; it was Paula. We stood there looking at each other, she was even whiter, even wearing a blond wig, and I must have been the same color as she, and her manner was delicate but her voice was firm. "Is there anything here that has special meaning for you?"

I put a chair on the table and retrieved her photo from the hole in the ceiling tiles. Sabrina would never think of that hiding place, especially after I told I'd seen a rat go into that hole. "Let's go," said Paula. When we opened the door to leave, Sabrina was there, and when she saw me with Paula it looked like she was going to faint. Paula looked at her the way you look at the girl bagging your groceries at the supermarket and headed for the stairs, leading me by the arm. Sabrina came out of her trance and chased after us. "You're leaving?" "Yes, have a good life." She threw herself on the ground and grabbed my leg with the metal pins, "Please, forgive me, don't leave me, I love you." Every step I took, I would drag Sabrina along the floor and she was howling like an animal and in the midst of the howls and moans begging, "Leave him with me, you're rich and can get any man you want, he's all I have in the world, for the love of God I'll do anything you want, I'll be your slave for the rest of my life, leave him with me," and when we got to the head of the stairs I jerked my leg free and Sabrina rolled down the steps and lay motionless by the door to the outside. I tried to revive Sabrina but she wasn't breathing. Paula felt her pulse and said "The poor girl's dead and we'd better get out of here, there's nothing we can do."

We got into the car and drove silently through the streets, silently entered the tunnel. There had been a moment when I wished for the deaths of Sabrina and Tim Maia, but it wasn't for real and I was dying of pity for her. "I'm sorry too," said Paula, "but it wasn't your fault, it wasn't my fault, it wasn't anyone's fault."

"I want to go back," I said, "I'm not going to leave her there, dead." Paula agreed. "All right, maybe it's best that way." The car stopped at the corner. "Tomorrow I'll come by in the afternoon, wait for me," and Paula left. There was a crowd at the door, curiosity-seekers, a policeman who said the meat wagon was on its way. Dona Alzira greeted me with an avalanche of words, "Ah, you're here, your friend fell down the stairs, I was watching television when I heard the noise and ran, I mean first I put on my robe, in this heat nobody stays fully dressed at home, and the outside door was open and the girl was lying there and I saw right away she was dead, I've seen lots of dead people in my time, I'm not a child, my dead sister's face was just like that girl's and the man from the police wants to talk to you." The policeman said only that I'd have to go to the precinct to make a statement. The onlookers left and Dona Alzira went off to watch her soap, leaving only the policeman and me and poor Sabrina, whose hair seemed even more bleached, to wait for the medical examiner and the meat wagon.

At the police station I told a pile of lies: I'd gone out to buy a newspaper and halfway there I realized I didn't have any money on me and I went back and found my girlfriend fallen at the foot of the stairs and Dona Alzira said she heard the noise and came out right away. "That's not exactly what Dona Alzira said," the detective said, "she said she went to put on some clothes and it took her some time and, another thing, why did the dead woman leave the door open, the upstairs one, was she in a hurry? Was she running? Where was she going?" I explained, "Sabrina probably, because she knew I didn't have the key with me, came down to open the outside door and slipped." "And who opened the lower door? It was already open. Did you two fight?" "Us? Never, she was a saint, you can ask Dona Alzira if we ever fought, I was going to marry her, she was a saint, she took care of me when I broke this leg here full of metal pins, she did physical therapy on me every day for I don't know how long, she was a saint." "When you're not married to them they're all saints," the detective said, and added that one of these days he'd want to question me again but for now I could go.

The next day Paula showed up in a blond wig and dark glasses. She said, "Listen, you're going to do some tests, I don't trust state-run hospitals," and she gave me a bunch of papers with orders for tests, there were tests of feces, urine, blood, electrical tests of heart and head, and she said the lab had instructions to carry out the tests and that I shouldn't worry about payment and that she'd be back in two weeks.

Two weeks later she returned, still in the wig and glasses, but she took the wig off right away and said that my tests had been very good and she took off the dark glasses and touched my leg and asked if the leg was hurting and my dick got hard, all those crisp new bills from the Mint. I said that what hurt was my heart, that I dreamed about her every night. We took off our clothes, her body was even whiter than I had imagined and her hair darker, and we fucked fucked fucked.

And we fucked fucked fucked the next day all afternoon and every day that week, all afternoon, and on Friday she said she'd only see me again on Monday and asked if I was like that with other women too. I was no fool and gave her my word of honor that it had never happened with me before, she was what made it happen, I liked her, loved her, was crazy about her, liked her the way a child likes chocolate ice cream and loved her the way a mother loves her child and was crazy mad in love with her and that was why I fucked her like a tiger fucks a wildcat. And we would laugh during breaks and eat grilled cheese sandwiches with Coca-Cola and I wasn't lying, with the other women it was a mere rebound from the crackling bills from the Mint but with Paula it was passion, it pained elevated inspired bled. "We can't tell anyone about this," she told me, and that would be the last thing in the world that I would do, I knew she was married to the owner of the bank where I had worked and she knew that I knew because her full name was printed beneath the newspaper photo and I'd die before I'd tell.

But I had to let off steam with someone, so I told the dwarf. I went out one weekend day thinking about her, missing her to death because I knew that Saturday and Sunday we wouldn't see each other, and then I saw the dwarf going through the garbage can of a luncheonette and he told me, as if to excuse his scavenging in the garbage, "Sometimes I score an almost whole sandwich, and life's not easy." I replied, "That's true," and showed him the laminated newspaper clipping with Paula's picture. "Helluva woman," he said. "Show more respect, you shitty dwarf." I grabbed him by the arm and shook and tossed the dwarf against a parked car and he looked so unhappy that I took pity on him and invited him to get some coffee. I showed him the picture again, "I'm deeply in love, I think about her day and night, she's as white as a lily," and the dwarf listened very attentively, giving small grunts as dwarfs like to do, that dwarf at least.

Paula would invent things, she brought an enormous oilcloth that she put on top of the mattress and every day she would bring something, olive oil, the kind of tomato sauce you use on spaghetti, molasses, milk, and order me to slather it on our naked bodies and we'd fuck on the oilcloth. And we laughed in between and fucked a little more under the shower and on top of the table, her sitting on the edge with her legs open and me standing up. One day she brought a Polaroid camera to take pictures of my dick and I took pictures of her pussy and her ass and her breasts and her face, which was the part of her that turned me on most of all, and then we tore up all the pictures. All but one, of her nude and smiling at me, which I didn't have the heart to tear up.

Every Saturday I would meet the dwarf and buy him lunch with the money from my unemployment insurance and the dwarf would listen, grunting, to me saying how much in love I was, how Paula was the most beautiful woman in the world, how one day I'd done it nine times and come every time and her too, and that she'd go home with her legs aching. "Women have strong legs," said the dwarf, but I don't think he believed what I was saying. That Saturday I monopolized the dwarf the entire day, and that night we went to dinner and got smashed and I took the dwarf to where he lived, not far from my house, in a shack in the slums near Piranhão, the headquarters of the municipal government, so called because it was once the whorehouse district. When I woke up, Paula's pictures, the one from the newspaper and the Polaroid, had vanished, and I was desperate and went to the place where we'd gotten drunk but nobody had found the photos and I went to the dwarf's shack and he wasn't there and I spent the rest of Sunday in desperation and the entire night awake banging my head against the wall.

On Monday Paula showed up and didn't take off her wig or the dark glasses or put down her purse or give me a kiss and said, "Some guy named Haroldo called my home this morning and claimed he was your friend and that he had a photo of me naked and said he wanted money to return the photo. Did you keep one of those photos?" I got down on my knees in front of her and begged for forgiveness and kissed her shoe and said it was that shitty dwarf and told her everything and asked for forgiveness again and I remembered Sabrina dragging on my leg with the pins in it. "What now? What are we going to do?" said Paula. "Leave it to me," I said, and Paula left, and when she left without having taken off the wig, without have set down her purse, without having removed the dark glasses, and without kissing me, I rolled on the floor like a mad dog cursing that sonofabitch of a dwarf.

I went looking for the dwarf where he hung out and when he saw me he tried to run and I said, "Take it easy, man, I'm here to tell you it's a done deal, the lady's going to give you the dough you want, or rather, she's going to pay double and half goes to me, agreed?" "You're not pissed at me? Really?" "You're my brother, man, bring the pictures to my place tonight and the lady'll give you the dough." We shook hands solemnly like two businessmen and I left and walked down Constituição Street and bought an old leather suitcase and got home and rolled on the floor some more and foamed at the mouth like an epileptic.

The dwarf arrived at eight-thirty and seeing me alone in the living room asked, "Where's the woman?" I pointed to the closed bedroom door and said, "She's in there and doesn't want to talk to you, give me the photos in exchange for the dough," and he gave me the photos, the one from the newspaper and the one of her nude, pretty, smiling at me. I grabbed the dwarf by the throat and lifted him into the air and he thrashed and made me stagger around the room, bumping into the furniture, until we fell to the floor and I put my knees on his chest and squeezed until my hands ached and I saw he was dead. And then I squeezed his throat again and put my ear against his chest to see if his heart was beating and I squeezed again and again and again and spent the rest of the night squeezing his throat. When day broke I placed him in the suitcase and opened the window and breathed the morning air with the eagerness with which I sipped the air coming from Paula's mouth when we fucked.

The next day Paula arrived and I gave her the photos, the one from the paper too, and said, "Everything's taken care of, don't worry," and she ripped up the two photos into tiny little pieces and put it all in her bag and stood there with the bag in her hand and the glasses on her face and the wig on her head and didn't kiss me and said, "I'm pregnant by my husband, by my husband, by my husband, I think it best if we don't see each other again," and she looked at the suitcase and dashed out.

I was alone, without the woman I loved madly, without Sabrina who was buried in Caju cemetery, and without the only friend I'd had in the world, who was the dwarf inside the suitcase, and night came and since I didn't have her picture anymore I sat there looking at the suitcase till daybreak, when I picked up the suitcase and with it paced back and forth in the room.

THE FLESH AND THE BONES

My plane wasn't leaving till the next day. For the first time, I regretted not having a picture of my mother with me, but I'd always thought it was idiotic to go around with family pictures in your pocket, especially a picture of your mother.

I didn't mind spending two more days wandering the streets of that vast, dirty, polluted anthill that was full of strange people. It was better than walking around a small city, with pure air and bumpkins who say hello when you pass by. I'd stay there a year if I didn't have an obligation waiting for me.

I walked all day, breathing the carbon monoxide. At night my host invited me to dinner. A woman accompanied us.

We ate worms, the most expensive dish at the restaurant. When I looked at one of them on the tip of my fork, it seemed to me like the kind of larva or botfly pupa that lose their black hairs and milky color when they're fried. It was a rare worm, they explained to me, that is extracted from a vegetable. If it were a botfly, it would be even more expensive, I answered, ironically. I've had botflies in my body three times, twice in the leg and once in the belly, and my horses and my dogs have also had them. It's hard to get the whole thing out so it can be fried—it could only be tasty like these if it was fried—and eaten. I crammed my mouth with worms.

Afterward, we went to a place that my host wanted to show me.

The spacious club had a runway, where women paraded naked, dancing or posing, at its center. We made our way through the tables; they were filled with men in ties. We ordered something from the waiter, then took our place. Beside us, a woman in nothing but a cache-sexe, on all fours, was rubbing her buttocks against the pubis of a man in a coat and tie, who was sitting with his legs spread. Her expression was neutral, and the man, a guy of about forty, looked as peaceful as if he were ensconced in a barber's chair. The overall effect reminded me of a modern art installation. A few days earlier, in another city, in another country, I had gone to an art gallery to see a dead pig rotting inside a glass box. As I was in the city for only a few days, I only got to see the animal turn greenish; they told me it was too bad I couldn't contemplate the work in all its transcendent power, with worms eating the flesh.

The exhibition in the cabaret also struck me as metaphysical, like the sight of the dead pig in its shining glass enclosure. The woman reminded me, for one short moment, of a gigantic toad, because she was squatting and because her face, mulatto or Indian, had something of the amphibian. Three other men were at the table; they pretended to take no notice of the woman's movements.

We couldn't see everything that was going on in the room from our table. But at the tables around us there were always one or two women who were moored to a fully clothed man. The admission ticket entitled us to have one of the innumerable women—who performed strip teases at various places in the room—rub against us. There was a choreographic pattern to the caresses: the woman would go down on all fours, rub her buttocks against the pubis of the man, who remained seated in his chair, then dance in front of him. Some of the more assiduous women would climb on top of a guy and pin his face between their thighs. Then they would take the admission ticket and leave.

The only woman watching the spectacle was our companion. My host called her Countess; I don't know if that was her name or her title. When I was young I knew a woman who told me she was a real countess, but I think it was a lie. Anyway, I called my tablemate Ms. Countess, the way I used to do with the other one. She watched what was going on around us and smiled discreetly, behaving like an adult at a circus was supposed to.

From every corner came the loud sound of dance music. To be able to speak to the Countess, I had to bring my mouth close to her ear. I said something that distinguished me as a dispassionate and bored observer; I forget what it was. With her mouth almost glued to my ear, the Countess, after commenting on the actions of a woman near us, who was rubbing her pussy in the face of a man in a bowtie, quoted, in Latin, Terence's well known saying: nothing human was alien to her and therefore she wasn't frightened. And to demonstrate it, she moved her body to the rhythm of the reverberating sound and sang the lyrics of one of the songs. And I accompanied her, beating time on the table.

There was a glass shower stall, brightly illuminated by spotlights, in the room in which the women took turns bathing. Some wet and washed their entire body, soaping ankles, pubes, knees, elbows, hair. Others performed stylized ablutions. "They're saying, 'I'm clean, trust me,'" the Countess whispered into my ear.

We waited for the drawing. The winner could choose any of the women to spend the rest of the night with, as the master of ceremonies explained.

We, my host and I, weren't drawn. The Countess hadn't bought a raffle ticket.

Then we all fell silent, without singing or keeping time to the music on the tabletop. We paid—the host paid—and left.

We said goodbye on the sidewalk in front of the bar. The Countess offered to drop me off at the hotel. And the host. I said I wanted to walk a bit; great cities are very pretty at sunrise.

I had been walking for about ten minutes, regretting not having a photo of my mother in my pocket, or in an album, or in a drawer, when the Countess's car pulled up beside me.

"Get in," she said. "I feel like crying and don't want to cry alone."

When we got to the hotel there was a message from my

brother. I called him from the room. The Countess heard the conversation with my brother. "I'm very sorry," she said, sitting on the bed, covering her face with her hands, "but I'm not crying for you, I'm crying for me."

I lay down on the bed and looked at the ceiling. She lay beside me. She rested her damp cheek against mine and said fucking was a way of celebrating life. We fucked in silence and then showered together; she imitated one of the women at the cabaret by washing and singing, and I accompanied her by tapping on the walls of the shower. She said she was feeling better and I said I was feeling better.

I caught the plane.

Nine and a half hours later I arrived at the hospital.

My mother's body was in the chapel, in a coffin covered with flowers, on a catafalque. My brother was smoking beside it. There was no one else.

"She asked for you a lot," my brother said. "So I went up to her and said I was you; she grasped my hand tightly, said your name, and died."

The remains of my father and my brother were already in the family resting place. A cemetery worker said that someone would have to be there for the exhumation. I went. My brother seemed more tired than me.

There were four exhumations. They opened the pink marble gravestone and hammered the cement plate that covered the tomb to pieces. The gravesite was divided in two by a slab. One of the gravediggers went down into the open hole, carefully, so as not to step on the remains of my brother, which were in the upper part. My brother's clothes were in good condition. He had good teeth, the molars were filled with gold. When the head was removed, the lower jaw came loose from the rest of the skull. The femur and tibia were more or less intact; the ribs looked like brown cardboard.

The gravediggers tossed the bones into a white plastic box that was next to the grave. Three cockroaches and a red centipede climbed up the walls; the centipede appeared faster than the roaches, but the roaches vanished first. I said in a loud voice that the centipede was poisonous. The gravedigger, or whatever he was called, paid no attention to what I had said.

As soon as my brother's remains were placed in the plastic box, his name was written in large letters on the lid. One of the men got into the grave and used a hammer and chisel to break the slab that enclosed the lower part, where the remains of my father, who had died two years before my brother, were found. The exhumer got back into the grave. My father's bones were in bad shape; some of them were so crumbled they looked like earth. Everything was thrown into another plastic box and mixed with remains of fabric; my father's clothes weren't as good as my brother's and had rotted as much as the bones. The only thing left from my father's skull was his false teeth; the red acrylic of the dentures shone more than the centipede.

I gave the guys a good tip. The two boxes were placed beside the tomb.

I went back to the chapel.

My brother was smoking and gazing through the window at the traffic outside.

A priest appeared and prayed.

The closed casket was placed on a cart. The gravedigger dragged the cart to the open grave and we, my brother and I, followed. My mother's coffin was placed in the lower part. A slab was cemented in place, leaving the upper part empty, awaiting its future occupant. The two boxes with the remains of my father and my brother were deposited over the slab, temporarily. The pink marble gravestone with the names of the two, carved in bronze, closed the tomb.

They must have stolen the gold fillings from my brother's teeth when I went to the chapel to get my mother, I thought. But I was too tired to comment on it. We walked in silence to the gate of the cemetery. My brother hugged me. "Want a lift?" he asked. I said I was going to walk a bit. I watched the car pull away. I stayed there, standing, until it grew dark.

Rubem Fonseca is one of Brazil's most influential writers and was awarded the Prémio Camões—considered the Nobel Prize of Portuguese language literature—for his body of work in 2003. That same year he was awarded the Juan Rulfo Prize. He is the author of eight novels, including *High Art*, *Vast Emotions and Imperfect Thoughts*, and *Bufo & Spallanzani*, all of which have been published in English translation. One of his famous characters is Mandrake, a cynical and amoral lawyer and the basis for an HBO series of the same name.

Clifford E. Landers has translated over twenty book-length works from Portuguese, including novels by Rubem Fonseca, Jorge Amado, João Ubaldo Ribeiro, Patrícia Melo, José de Alencar, Chico Buarque, Paulo Coelho, António Lobo Antunes, and Marcos Rey. He is the author of *Literary Translation: A Practical Guide*, published by Multilingual Matters Ltd. in 2001. He received the Mario Ferreira Award in 1999 and a National Endowment for the Arts translation grant in 2004.

Open Letter—the University of Rochester's nonprofit, literary translation press—is one of only a handful of publishing houses dedicated to increasing access to world literature for English readers. Publishing twelve titles in translation each year, Open Letter searches for works that are extraordinary and influential, works that we hope will become the classics of tomorrow.

Making world literature available in English is crucial to opening our cultural borders, and its availability plays a vital role in maintaining a healthy and vibrant book culture. Open Letter strives to cultivate an audience for these works by helping readers discover imaginative, stunning works of fiction and by creating a constellation of international writing that is engaging, stimulating, and enduring.

Current and forthcoming titles from Open Letter include works from France, Norway, Brazil, Lithuania, Iceland, and numerous other countries.

www.openletterbooks.org